LE TOM'S

CAFÉ UNFILTERED

JEAN-PHILIPPE BLONDEL

TRANSLATED FROM THE FRENCH
BY ALISON ANDERSON

NEW VESSEL PRESS
NEW YORK

The translator would like to thank
Alexandra Hudson for her assistance.

New Vessel Press

www.newvesselpress.com

First published in French in 2022 as *Café sans filtre*
Copyright © Éditions de l'Iconoclaste, 2022

This edition is published by arrangement with Éditions de l'Iconoclaste
in conjunction with its duly appointed agent,
Books and More Agency #BAM, Paris, France. All rights reserved.

Translation Copyright © 2023 Alison Anderson

Library of Congress Cataloging-in-Publication Data
Blondel, Jean-Philippe
[Café sans filtre. English]
Café Unfiltered/ Jean-Philippe Blondel; translation by Alison Anderson.
p. cm.
ISBN 978-1-954404-20-5

Library of Congress Control Number: 2022950143
I. France—Fiction

To my wife and my daughters, for everything.
To Sylvie and Chloé, for inspiration.
To Jacob, Alberto, Christophe, Jean-Claude, Christine,
Laurent, Géraldine, and Anaïs, for a life spared.
To everyone who came walking with me along Les Viennes
during this strange interlude:
Jean-Marc, Nelly, Franck, Laurent, Yasmine, Fabien,
Cécile, Valérie, JP, Claude, Willy, Isabelle P.,
Isabelle W., Olivier F., Élisabeth, Olivier D., Jacqueline,
Gilles, Véronique M., Fabienne, Bastien,
and to Pascale for her daily phone calls.

And then, to Suzanne Vega, naturally.

"Take heart, we're all connected,
but we forget to remember."
Nicolas Bouvier, *The Japanese Chronicles*

9:00 A.M.

CHLOÉ FOURNIER, 31 YEARS OLD—TABLE NO. 8

(room at the back, to the left, by the picture window)

I'M A PARASITE.

That's precisely what José the waiter must think of me. He claps his napkin over his shoulder and lets out an exasperated sigh, but he hasn't threatened to throw me out yet. Honestly, that would be ridiculous: in all the time I've been seeking refuge here, the room has never been more than half full.

Customers may have started coming back inside, but they're uneasy. They keep their mask within reach, and finger it nervously. The limit imposed on gatherings has been lifted, and if we want, we can get together in groups of twelve or fifteen. What's worrying is this new variant everyone's talking about, with a Greek letter for a name, but it makes you think of India all the same—majestic elephants, Bollywood, and overcrowded cities.

The terrace, on the other hand, is often packed with people. They've heard that there's virtually no risk out in the fresh air, that droplets are dispersed on the wind and won't contaminate our skin. Droplets, too, have been let out of confinement, have become immaterial. Still, people remain discreet when it comes to laughter and exclamations. And at the end of the tunnel. People squinting. Groping for the daylight. All these curfews have accustomed us to behaving like pet mice. At night we scurry around at home, without sticking our nose outside.

It's the same when it comes to conversation. It's often *mezza voce*, for fear of arousing the demons of Wuhan or elsewhere. We mutter the word "vacation" tentatively, and at the same time make a face that means: Like last year, our vacation won't be anything like it used to be. Wait and see. All of us, wait and see.

Except me.

Sitting on my leatherette banquette, I'm not waiting for anything. I'm observing. The way men and women behave. The ones who used to greet each other with open arms, and now they touch each other's shoulder or upper arm, sometimes daring to let a hand linger on the other's skin, until they withdraw their fingers, furtively, and rack their brains wondering where they've left the hand sanitizer.

Now and again our gazes meet. They realize I'm staring at them and they move a few inches away. I'm making them uneasy. Then they spot my notebooks and pencils, and the big fountain pen, and they breathe more easily. An artist. The satisfaction of being able to pigeonhole me. Ah yes, the arts. Culture. Fields that have suffered more than others, over the last two years, right? So abruptly deprived of an audience and their only source of income. How are we going to make it through these times? It's almost as if they're about to give me a few euros, along with some words of compassion and encouragement. *We are all with you. We believe in you.*

I wonder how much they'll remember, once they look away. The image that's been printed on their retina. A woman in her thirties. Her hair on the short side. Straight. Brown, almost black. The color of her eyes? Green? Blue? Brown? No, honestly, now, they haven't been paying attention. Nor to her figure—which must mean there's nothing worthy of note where that's concerned. Especially as she was sitting down, you see. It's always tricky trying to gauge a person's height when they're not standing there in front of you. She had a nose piercing, didn't she? Or maybe it's just what you expect from an artist, it's such a cliché, with artists. Oh yes, because she's most definitely an artist. She was sketching. The streets nearby. The interior of the bar. Who knows, maybe when I first noticed her she was sketching my portrait. I'd really like to see that. If I run into her again, I'll ask her. Except that if I do run into her, I won't recognize her. In the meantime, she'd do better to find another occupation. A real job, in other words.

I think about all the places I've worked. The offices in Paris. The company with an open-plan layout in Helsinki. The tearoom in Vantaa. The convenience store next to my parents' place. After all these years waiting on other people, going through their lives, all I want now is peace and quiet. *To step aside.* That's it. That's the right way to put it. Since the autumn, I've stepped *aside.* As I had already cut myself off from the rest of the world a few months earlier, when I came home from Vantaa, I've become marginal. No, that's not right. I'm on the red line separating the margin from the rest of the page. It's a rope I've stretched tight and I'm walking on it, clumsily. I don't know when I'll fall and whether it will all end badly. Above all, for the time being it doesn't interest me.

It's other people who captivate me. All the people my age, making their way, fearful or bold, convinced they've been through the most intense time in their life during these various lockdowns, and that they're rediscovering a world that they'd taken for granted. I find them touching, and I envy them as well. Though you might not think it, I'd like to join in the dance again, too, but I've forgotten the steps.

Oh, there goes the bell on the door—a relic connecting this café to bygone places—nineteenth-century grocery shops, village bakeries. A new customer. I like the way they hesitate in the doorway, as if they have to wait for permission from the master of the house before entering his private space. Outside, there's a sudden rumbling. Clouds have massed in a corner of the sky. I didn't know the forecast was for storms. I don't listen to the weather report anymore.

THIBAULT DETRESSANT, 57—TABLE NO. 2
(first row on the right, picture window)

I HATE BEING the first to arrive at a meeting, yet I'm systematically five or ten minutes early. It's my father's fault.
He worked for the national rail company and always made
us respect schedules—which meant more or less hanging
around for over twenty minutes in the station waiting room
or on the platform, the time it took for the train to conde-
scend to show its face. I can still see my mother, like a priest-
ess in her suit and beige raincoat, hair in a chignon, while
her husband chatted with his colleagues on the platform.
No one paid any attention to me. They knew I was obedient. I wasn't about to start running around and jumping
across the tracks. I would probably make a career as a civil
servant like my father, with an inclination for rail transport. What they hoped was that I'd attain a position slightly
superior to my old man's. That was how upward mobility
worked, wasn't it? To do this I would probably have to exile
myself in the capital. In the average, provincial town where
we lived, the prospects for advancement were limited. And
besides, they needed young people who were full of ambition, who would steer the Grand Old Locomotive toward

new horizons. The number of pontificating speeches I used to have to listen to . . .

I recall that it was at moments like that, when we'd be waiting on the platform for the Mulhouse-Paris train to pull in, that I most regretted being an only child. With a brother, or even a sister, I could have shared things. Talked. Squabbled. Anyway. Here's what's left, half a century later: this unpleasant habit of waiting around, wondering if someone's not about to flake out on me. In the present case, it's unlikely. Pierre will show up, of course he will. I'm yawning in advance. There, too, I wonder what came over me, to accept his invitation. I really have to learn to say a flat no. I thought I'd made progress in that respect, thanks to my therapist. Well, to be completely honest, now I'm able to get around things, put people at a distance, and reply in the negative with a combination of firmness and politeness. But there are times I still get taken for a ride. On evenings when the solitude becomes too great. When memories get the upper hand. I hate myself for being so weak.

I really would have preferred to sit out on the terrace, but the weather's not right for it. Particularly as there's no one in the main room. Oh, yes, there is, a young girl sitting at a table at the back. She's got pencils and notebooks spread out in front of her. She must be a student from the Beaux-Arts. We used to make fun of them, Pierre and I, when we were still at the lycée, because they all went around dressed from head to toe in black, with a huge drawing portfolio tucked under one arm. That was a long time ago. I really shouldn't have agreed to this meeting.

He caught me off guard, at the worst moment and in the worst way, two nights ago. I had no plans that evening—with age, I have to admit, invitations have gotten scarcer, even for a local hero like me. I was scrolling through photos of other people's lives on Instagram and Facebook. I feel a certain tenderness toward Facebook, it's a network for old people who're convinced they can compete with the younger generation. All these people taking pictures of the meal they've ordered who write "yum," followed by four exclamation marks. All these quotes, half of them wrong, paired with reflections about the meaning of life. It's roughly the equivalent of those black-and-white photo romances my grandmother used to read in *Modes de Paris*.

I've been hitting the gin a shade too often. It's been happening more and more, lately, and I'm going to have to cut back on my consumption. It doesn't show yet, physically, because I look after myself, but the nightcap is tending toward a daily thing. And double. So I was feeling at a loose end just when Pierre posted the photo. It came onto the screen and I had to clench my jaw because right from the start I felt both sadness and rage.

We were both posing, an arm around each other's shoulder, at the edge of the park surrounding the lycée. We were trying to imitate Kerouac and Neal Cassady's pose, from a famous photo we'd come upon in the course of our reading. We were convinced we'd formed one of those inseparable friendships, like Castor and Pollux, Montaigne and La Boétie, Gatsby and Nick Carraway. A fine mess, that much was for sure.

The young woman—but maybe she's not all that young—has just looked up, and I'm afraid I might have said those last words out loud. It's been happening off and on, lately. I scare passersby. But they forgive me. I'm a writer, after all. And writers, it's a well-known fact, have foibles, and moments of brilliance. They don't stand on ceremony when it comes to attitude. Old eccentrics. One of those emblematic faces, whitened and powdered, that make people say when they see them, "He used to be famous, you know, that guy," and by "famous" they're also implying our energy, physical bearing, and readiness to raise hell.

Under no circumstances do I want to become any of that.

I was in love with Pierre. I try to sound detached, saying those words, to prove to my fictitious interlocutor that I've learned to keep my distance since those days. I've been trying, first and foremost, to convince myself that it's ancient history—like zip-neck sweaters, vinyl singles, and all those pins we cherished. I'll never part with the one I have of Bowie as Ziggy Stardust that I found at a secondhand clothing store during a school trip to Paris.

I was in love, but I never could have said those words at the time. I knew that there were men in the world who were attracted to other men. Certain films had popularized caricatures of them, and when they watched television my parents were torn between laughter and embarrassment. Because, well, really. It just isn't done, is it? I made my scorn for those characters clear, when they let out little shrieks and sported cigarette holders. I dragged myself around with shame in every pore; all the more so as Pierre came regularly to haunt my nights.

Yes, I was in love. It's been years since I've been obsessed with another man to the point of suffering physically from his absence. To the point of dreaming that he would die—a car crash, a fatal fall from a steep rock face leaving his corpse unrecognizable. Weeping profusely during the subsequent funeral. A promise never to forget, to become the immortalizer of the deceased hero. The shame of it.

And now it's the waiter's turn to look up. I smile vaguely to myself. I really am going to have to learn to keep these words from springing to my lips, which I mutter like the drunk I'm becoming.

I was in love and he wasn't. He was attracted to plucky girls who didn't hesitate to put him in his place, despite his good looks. He liked the fact they put up a resistance. And he loved the way I looked at him. A sort of idolatry that I couldn't repress. He knew very well what was going on, and he was toying with my attraction. He was even the first to suggest that we could share the same mattress or the same tent whenever we went to parties. Everyone else just saw us as inseparable. It seemed obvious that I'd eventually become the godfather of his children; oddly enough, no one imagined that I might have children myself someday, or might even want any.

And then one day I spoke with that girl. The one who took the photo. We'd seen each other around over the last few months. We were taking some of the same subjects. It was at one of those spur-of-the-moment parties and, for once, I was there without my sidekick. Oddly enough, he provided us with our first topic of conversation. Her name was Sophie. She wanted to be a psychologist. Out of the blue she asked me if I was sexually attracted to Pierre, and the whiskey and Coke I'd poured myself went down the wrong way, because in fact no one had ever spoken about him to me so openly, even though the corridors of the lycée were abuzz with insinuations. I looked out at the garden in the night: The host of the party—Laurence? Laurent?—had gone to a lot of trouble to decorate the place, with electric fairy lights, and lanterns among the trees; it was like theatre decor, it touched me. He or she had spent hours creating a backdrop that the guests hardly noticed. The words caught in my throat, even though I'd always taken myself for an insolent braggart. Sophie shook her head and came closer. She murmured in my ear that the answer was rather simple, in fact: Was he the one I thought about when I masturbated? I felt myself blush. She saw it, even in the half-light, and she touched my shoulder. She asked me if it was more pain than pleasure. I was staggered. She was eighteen, like us. How had she found the exact words, the ones that released tension yet rubbed salt in the wound all the while? Where had she gained such maturity? I asked her and she laughed. She wanted to study psychology and, rather than read theoretical books, since she didn't understand a thing at the moment, she had decided to observe her peers. Particularly Pierre and me, because there was this electricity between us, which she found nowhere else.

There was a moment of silence, riddled with shouts from the living room, where Yazoo's irresistible song "Don't Go" had just started. She lifted a strand of my hair and added, calmly, "You do know there's no hope."

I shrugged. There were tears in my eyes, I could have kicked myself. Somehow the word "yes" managed to make its way up my throat, to emerge in a croak. Sophie replied that if I knew that much, it wasn't so bad. What she found odd was the way he played with my desire. It must have flattered his ego—even men succumbed to his charm. She was sure that at some point, during sex, he sometimes called to me for help, to me and my vibrant desire, and that intensified his erection. I looked down. That was the first time I'd ever been so gently demolished. I felt Sophie's hand on my arm. Her advice was clear. Her advice was frank. *Go away.*

So I went away. I worked my guts out to improve my grades. I received my baccalaureate with honors. I was admitted to one of those elite programs in Paris, where my lack of culture would clash with the refinement and cruel courtesy of my classmates. My parents were proud of me, particularly my mother, she could picture me later in life as a professor of literature at the lycée—she used the words "literature professor" on purpose, it sounded so much classier than "French teacher"—on the condition, naturally, that I come back to my home town, and get married to another teacher (she'd be at the primary school, schoolmistress was a good job for a girl). I let her talk. I let all of them talk. Pierre, for a start, who couldn't get over the way my grades had suddenly skyrocketed. He had very mixed feelings about it all. He felt both proud and betrayed, admiring and scornful—and so, out of the blue, social success mattered to me after all?

I lied to him about my departure for Paris. He had promised to come to the station, but I didn't want to be subjected to the humiliation of waiting for him, only to realize just a few seconds before the train pulled in that, in the end, he wouldn't be coming. I didn't want my parents there, either. Or any other presence—except Sophie. She was there, smiling. She kept telling me to have faith. There would be good and bad surprises, but all of it was better than being stuck in this place, loving without hope of love in return, gradually going downhill.

I was that paralyzed figure standing on platform three. I was that boy who arrived in his room on the top floor of a Haussmann-era building, only to discover that he would be sharing the toilet and shower with the four other tenants on the landing. I was that nervous kid wandering through the streets in the Marais, or following a group of party boys, hoping he could join in—fearful all the while of catching that disease that was just beginning to spread and which was likened to a gay cancer.

I'm grimacing. I can just make out my reflection in the picture window. Whenever unpleasant memories resurface, my lip curls. All the insults I've swallowed. I thought they'd leave me in peace, at some point, but they still catch me unawares; all it takes is one photograph posted on social media.

When the picture came onto the screen, it made me sit back abruptly. So forty years later he still had to go and flaunt the relationship he once had with me. To blow his own trumpet. To show he's known some famous people. To make his life seem more beautiful. It was pathetic. He reappeared in my life when, through the local papers, he found out that I was coming back to settle in the town where I'd grown up, and he noticed that the local politicians had started showing themselves in my company. Instagram. Facebook. Even Snapchat. He tried everything—and one night, after too much alcohol, yet again—I gave in, and agreed to his virtual friendship.

He immediately flooded me with messages. He wanted to invite me over for dinner, introduce me to his wife and his daughters, well, when they were around, because now they were performing brilliantly at university, one in medical school and the other in engineering. He also wanted to reminisce about the time we'd spent together, which still seemed so recent to him, it had been a wonderful period, he found it hard to let it go sometimes, he would waffle on, and his daughters would roll their eyes and let out a sigh, oh yes, he'd already told them that anecdote, ha ha ha. Of course, he was very pleased with his life and he had visited a lot of countries during his vacations—he had an enviable position in an insurance company—he'd really liked Croatia, for example, but the US, on the other hand, in the end he'd never made it to the US, probably because we had promised each other we'd go there together, that famous trip to New York with you.

I read this verbal diarrhea, vacillating between pity and

dismay. I have a photographic memory. It often unsettles people around me, because I can recall very precise and intimate details—the shape of a scar, the color of a pair of trousers worn on a given day, the hue of the sky one evening at a party on the banks of the Seine. When I was still at the lycée, I didn't know what to do with my memory, cluttered as it was with trivia—the list of all the number one songs from 1977 on; the exact order of the tracks on the LP *Faith* by The Cure; the names of the various winners of the Prix Goncourt over the past ten years. I would've liked to scrap what was useless and experience the present moment to the fullest, but I couldn't.

Later, when I began to write novels, I understood how useful this storeroom-memory actually was. I didn't need to embark on lengthy research, or go through newspapers, or check old photo albums. Everything was there, ready to be used. And I can swear that nowhere, not in a single recess of my brain, is there the slightest reference to any trip to New York with Pierre. It's such a cliché. As the years went by, whenever he heard the song by Téléphone on the radio, he must have convinced himself that we, too, had wanted to share that experience. A gross chronological approximation. The album with that song only came out after I'd already been living in Paris for three years, and I'd had no more news either from him or from anyone else. I wasn't the one who failed to stay in touch. In the beginning I used to write to him—I'd given up on calling, I was awkward and ill at ease over the phone. I told him about my life, giving him a very toned-down version. I kept silent about the moments of intense despair, the depths of solitude I often fell into, and I shared only those anecdotes that just might make Pierre feel like joining me here once he had his vocational training certificate. All I got in response were two or three hastily written postcards of no interest. It didn't take me long to realize that Pierre and his crowd had moved on.

And now, suddenly decades later, this avalanche of messages. Initially I remained unmoved by his invitations—he wanted to introduce me to this or that restaurant that didn't exist "back in our day," or some bar where fiftysomethings were still welcome at night (double smiley). I could picture him telling his work colleagues that he'd known me since the dawn of time, that during our adolescence we'd been thick as thieves. One of them, mockingly, would surely mention my sexuality, something I've never kept hidden since moving to Paris. Instead of blushing, Pierre would give a laugh and probably come out with something like, "Yes, I think he was even a little in love with me, but what can you do, we don't choose our preferences."

I ignored him—until, of course, at one point I gave in. I wrote a few lines in reply. I even agreed once or twice to meet him for a drink—but not for long, okay, I insisted, just a quick one, because between writing my new novel, promoting the one that had just come out, and going back and forth to Paris all the time to meet the theatre directors who wanted to stage plays based on my work, I was swamped and had little time to spare.

And so, two nights ago I caved again. But this time was a bit different. It was not so much the photograph that upset me as the memory of the photographer. Sophie. I've realized that I really liked that girl. I should have tried to stay in touch. She was carried away on the current of promises not kept—the ones you make when you're in full transformation, shedding that youthful skin for good, along with its cumbersome burden of bitter experiences.

But that doesn't mean I've forgotten her. I thought about her quite often, about her and the influence she had on the course of my life, and she was one of the first people I looked for on the World Wide Web when it started invading our everyday lives. It was the end of the 1990s. There were constant rumors going around that the change of millennium would bring chaos. The planet would succumb to a huge global blackout that would probably lead to upheaval and a new era. Social media didn't exist yet, but it was still possible to look for traces of the luminaries we'd encountered. I remember spending entire evenings cross-checking information—true or false?—about men and women I'd spent time with or dreamed about. I didn't find Sophie right away. At first I figured she had probably gotten married and changed her name, in which case my investigation would hit a wall. And then I remembered her younger sister, whom I'd met briefly three or four times and had comforted on the evening of that memorable party. She'd been crying, because none of Sophie's friends would take her seriously. They treated her like a child, which was what she was, in fact. Listening to her complain and fret impatiently had distracted me from my own sorrows. When I was leaving, she told me she'd never forget my kindness. I gave a smile—hollow words. How wrong I was.

Her name lingered in a recess of my memory. Virginie. Apparently she was on the administrative staff of a science faculty in Paris—a management position, no less. Next to her name there was a portrait, where I could still see traces of the little girl she'd once been, and an email address. For several weeks I toyed with the idea of contacting her, then one evening I sent a few cryptic lines. I apologized right from the start: it wasn't very elegant to use her as an intermediary to ask for news of her sister. As it happened, I lied: I had recently come upon some photos of that bygone era when we all lived in the same town, and I'd gotten a yearning for news of my ghosts, her sister being one of them, and Virginie herself, actually, because of that discussion we'd had, the two of us, about the frustrations of being seen as insignificant, when all we dreamed of was being part of the crowd. It's something I've often felt in life myself, and every time, I'd remember her and the rage she expressed that night.

For several weeks there was no answer to my message, and I had to face facts—either I'd written to the wrong person, or Virginie didn't feel like bringing up past history. Nostalgia is a dangerous treacle, and not many people enjoy losing themselves in it.

And yet almost a month later, I saw Virginie's name in my inbox. In a short, dense paragraph she wrote that she'd taken some time to get back to me because she didn't understand what I wanted, in fact, and she didn't know how best to broach the subject. The sorrow was still too raw. Sophie had died three years earlier, from a poorly treated throat infection. She came down with a fever. She didn't see the point in going to the doctor's for so little. Her ex-husband had their two children that week. She took an aspirin. During the night her condition suddenly worsened. She could hardly breathe, and probably had trouble getting to the phone. By the time she finally managed to call for help it was already too late. She died at the hospital forty-eight hours later, without ever regaining consciousness. Virginie told me where she was buried, if ever I wanted to visit her grave. She realized that so much information coming all at once must be a shock, and that was why she had hesitated to write. Maybe it would have been better to leave me in the dark. But she remembered it so well, our conversation that night in the garden. And certain sentences from my novels, too. She'd read nearly all of them. She thought she recognized herself in one or two characters, but that was an illusion all readers shared, wasn't it? She would have loved to meet me but just then it was impossible. She was with her husband in Taiwan, enjoying the leisurely life of an expatriate wife, left much of the time to her own devices. In any case she'd let me know the next time she was back in France, we might meet for a coffee, to remember her sister together; she so rarely had the opportunity to speak about her. Her ex-brother-in-law and his children had severed all ties with her entire family. She had no idea how her nephew and niece were doing. She finished with a "Best regards," which seemed to clash with the rest of the message. We never did get back in touch.

That's it; it was Sophie I thought about, and her sister, too, when the photo appeared on my Facebook wall the day before yesterday. About Sophie and that grotesque death—how could anyone still die from a benign infection at the end of the twentieth century? About the woman who had taken the picture, and not the people posing for the lens. With the passage of time, actors have come to interest me less and less; it's the production that fascinates me. I've been reproached for favoring plot over characters in my recent novels. It's probably true.

I wasn't thinking, two nights ago, I hit the *like* button. It's strange how, over the last decade, this word "like" in English has crept into our conversations in French. *"J'ai liké."* What did I *like* about that portrait of Pierre and me, and in that wink sent from beyond the grave by a young woman who had altered the course of my existence?

Naturally, on the other side of the screen, Pierre quivered with joy. For once I was reacting to one of his posts! He immediately wrote a few lines to express his joy. Then he sent a voice message. He suggested we meet for a coffee. He said he'd just found this photo in a box in the attic, and there were others. He could bring them and then he'd scan the ones I chose. We could meet at his place or at mine. That is, if I wasn't too busy, of course—he supposed I had plenty of appointments with people who were far more interesting than he was.

Maybe it was that last sentence, which he added after a faint sigh, that made me yield. I've always had a soft spot for people who admit defeat. And so I replied, in writing. I hate those voice messages, which oblige phone users to hold their device horizontally while they share their conversation with everyone around them. I suggested we meet at a café. Out on the terrace, if possible, since that would make everyone feel more at ease, given these rumors about variants that were going around, once again. I pretended I was very busy the next day, with various meetings already scheduled and impossible to change, but I threw him a line for the following day. Thursday. At Le Tom's. I passed by there every morning and I've been promising myself I'd stop off one day. There was a spacious, pleasant terrace, with trees protecting it from the sun; there was the trickle of a nearby fountain, and the square, and the church of Saint-Urbain a few yards from there. Not exactly the town's nerve center, but almost. Closer to nine o'clock, when they opened. It would certainly be quieter. As I expected, he agreed to everything. An excellent idea, he added. He had never been to Le Tom's, either, this would be the opportunity. The opportunity for what, I wonder.

I didn't expect it to rain, and now it's pouring. Nor did I expect him to be late. I didn't think I'd be the only customer, apart from the gray mouse at the back, furtively glancing at me—yet another person who recognizes my face but can't "place me." A friend of her parents'? A shopkeeper? A local politician?

I'm sitting at the first table on the left. The banquette is not very comfortable. I'm right up against the window. The downpour is something else. At least I'm under cover. When the waiter comes over, I order a cup of Earl Grey. With a slice of lemon, please. Thank you.

CHLOÉ

A ROTTEN SUMMER. We'd expected everything but this.

The storm has broken. A phenomenal cloudburst Farther north, some cities have been flooded more than once, and the rescue services can hardly keep up. Here they keep a lookout on the rivers. They could flood the fields. Ruin the harvest. That's the last thing we need. To be in danger right in our own homes when for months we've been ordered to seek refuge there.

The picture window is vibrating from the onslaught. I feel good here. I wonder how this café has survived, what with the lockdown, then reopening to half-capacity and curfews. I wonder how I would have managed all this, in Vantaa. But maybe in Finland the rules were not as strict. I haven't kept up. I wanted as little news as possible. All I have is names. Annika and Ari, of course. Mrs. Virtanen. Names like bandages, torn off. No. I won't look at the wound. There's no point.

I heard that the Swedes didn't react the same way as the rest of Europe, and that they're trying to obtain herd immunity. For the time being they're letting the most vulnerable people die in the hospital. It's a cynical way of handling the problem of retirement, though you wouldn't think it, even if no one would stake their life on the truth of it. Natural selection, Nordic version. Either you're born to overcome the hardship of life in the Arctic—you're tall, vigorous, and healthy, and you refuse to complain, so you deserve to survive; or you're cut from a different cloth and in that case, good luck.

Don't get me wrong. I loved living in Vantaa, just outside Helsinki. I even thought I'd spend the rest of my life there. I hadn't planned to get on a plane last year at the beginning of March, to come back here with my red suitcase and stay all alone for weeks on end in my parents' house. Well, my mother's house, since my father died ten years ago now. Virtually no one's house, really, since my mother lives in the south of France with a beekeeper she met on the Meetic dating site. My mother thought about selling the place. She asked me for my opinion, of course. I didn't have one. Time dragged on—and then all of a sudden, that suburban-style house from the 1960s with its little flower beds and vegetable garden became my refuge. My mother was glad to have someone looking after it during lockdown. She was afraid squatters might move in and ruin everything. Squatters. In this housing project at the edge of town, where all the streets are named after famous composers. Mozart. Schumann. Schubert. I live on rue Satie.

I would have liked painters' names better. Vermeer. Leonardo da Vinci. Mondrian. Bacon. Although rue Bacon—that's sort of pushing it, isn't it? Let's just say I would have felt more at home there. I glance at my things spread out on the table. My pencils. My sketchbooks. They're useful here. They act as a shield. You can't decently throw someone out if they're settled at a table to work—particularly in the era of coworking.

I doodle. I erase. I add details. Colored lines. Gradually the picture starts coming together. I'm pleased with it. Unravel the tension. That's my sole aim. I'm not trying to create a work of art. That would be a waste of time. The thing as a whole is still awkward, sometimes naive, but I've noticed that I'm making progress: the room at Le Tom's is beginning to resemble, on paper, what it seems to be, to me. Two rooms separated by three steps. Nine tables. The counter, on the right as you come in: that's José's sanctum, he's the waiter, with his suppressed anger. Fabrice's sanctum, too; he's the owner. They're the ones I should begin to sketch now. To liven up the place. To fill my existence.

I've known Fabrice since secondary school. We were in Spanish class together. He was really good at it. He often comes in later in the morning, and stays until evening. Clearly, he hasn't recognized me, he's barely said a word to me. I'd like to draw the young woman who helps in the kitchen at lunch—I think her name is Ifemelu. She has a magnificent forehead. Yesterday she was looking for dessert recipes. I felt like slipping her the recipes for the cakes I used to make in Vantaa. But I didn't. There's no point. Another story. Another geography.

I don't want to think about all that anymore. I don't want to go back to being the woman I once was, and I have no idea what sort of woman I might become. For a year and a half now I've been caught in a sort of suspended present, and I can't get out of it. Sometimes I picture myself stuck in an airplane that's stalled ten thousand feet above the ground; the crew and the other passengers have all disappeared, and I can't get into the cockpit. Time has come to a standstill. The only thing I can do is jump. I've found a parachute, but I don't know how to use it.

While waiting to make a decision, I would rather immerse myself in the lives of others. In only a few days Le Tom's has become the nest I had despaired of ever finding, even though José consistently tries to kick me out. I slip into the skin of the people I'm sketching. It's easy and, more than anything, restful. I've never found anything more relaxing than escaping my own life and projecting myself into the lives of complete strangers. I borrow someone's body, someone's mind, and off I go. And even though world geography is tangled up in health regulations, and moving around has become restricted, I can escape with disconcerting ease.

I focus on the handful of morning customers. That man who came in a little while ago, just before the downpour. His face looks vaguely familiar. He's getting impatient, he checks his watch every thirty seconds, and yet he stays put. Now he's sitting up straight because someone is coming in the door, but then right away he slumps: It's clearly not the person he was waiting for. It's a couple. A surprising pair: a woman in her fifties and a young man, who could be her son, apart from the fact that he doesn't really look like her. She's shooting fearful little glances from left to right. Drops of rain are trickling from her hair down her neck and onto her back, and she's trying not to shiver. She is not, or is no longer, in the habit of coming to places like this. As for the young man, he's in his element, and he's laughing at their recent misadventure. They thought they could avoid the downpour, but boom, the clouds burst before they even had time to say phew. He is discreetly pushing the woman toward the nearest empty table; the number 3 is carved on a little bronze plaque. He calls to the waiter. Using his first name. He asks if the boss is anywhere around, and then he answers his own question with a forced laugh: of course not, he must still be lounging in bed, oh man, a good thing José is there to keep the place going. José doesn't even look up. The young man goes on talking, happy to hear his own voice echoing through the room, proud to be filling this space normally reserved for mezza voce conversations. Finally he turns to speak to the woman, who sat down, very straight, on the banquette, once she'd hung her raincoat on the coatrack. I eavesdrop on their conversation.

"What will you have, Maman? Green tea? Coffee for me. A double espresso, even. I really need it, after getting drenched like that."

"Black."

"Pardon?"

"The tea. Black. English Breakfast, if you've got it."

José nods, discreetly. He'll bring a little wooden box where dozens of packets of tea are arranged in rows, and she'll choose. Suddenly this makes me feel like having some. I, too, would gladly order a cup of tea. Served in a big teapot, not one of those ridiculous stainless steel receptacles you burn your fingers on, with hardly enough liquid to fill the cup. A real, hefty, porcelain teapot, of the kind that sits there while the hours go by. I doubt they have one like that in stock. That's a mistake. It was in part because I offered that sort of English tea service that I gained a loyal clientele. *My clientele.* The word makes me smile. Smile, then grimace. As usual. No, honestly. Stop dwelling on all that. Take your distance. Pick up a pencil, instead. Perfect the details. There. That's good. Feel the peace and quiet return. Glance over at the newcomers. Start a portrait. Furtively.

GUILLAUME, 25—TABLE NO. 3

BLACK. Well well, I was convinced she drank only green tea. But it's true that lately, she's been taking a malicious pleasure in confusing the issue. Who would have thought. My mother, being original. My mother, changing her habits. My mother, becoming different. There's an incompatibility between those words. An oxymoron. That's it, that's what it's called. An opposition that catches your attention, snappy as a slogan. A photograph of my mother, and underneath, in red, these words: "A woman who's different." That would be first-rate, like a teaser. I can already see the trailer. She's walking down the street. She's shoving everything out of her way. You can sense her determination. She refuses to play by the rules currently in force. She'd be irresistible, for marketing perfume, for example. Or luxury prêt-à-porter. Hey, that's a great oxymoron, too.

I can't believe it, how sidetracked I can get! Just because my mother asked for black tea instead of green. Okay, in actuality that's not the only reason. There's something weird going on with her lately. My father's worried. He urged her to get her blood checked and go for some tests.

"She laughed in my face." That's what he told me last night when we were discussing the situation. And the very notion that my mother could laugh at my father's advice upsets me more than I would have thought. My mother doesn't laugh in people's faces. My mother gets up in the morning, humming, making breakfast, cutting a few stems from the bouquet my father gave her last Saturday. Then she gets busy. Doing what, I have no idea. Household chores, even though Rosa already comes twice a week. She also spends an hour at her fitness club at the top of the street. She has her meditation apps. She's been bored, I suppose, ever since my sister and I flew the nest—but there's nothing to be done. That's life, after all. Personally I think she ought to find a job. Something part time, in an interior decoration place, where she could lavish sensible advice on the customers. A few nights ago I came upon a program about professions that are enjoying a boom. Influencer. Content producer. One of the women interviewed was a conversation coach—in fact, she organized seminars where she told her clients what subjects they should bring up during their dinner parties, so that the guests would go away again that evening with the impression they'd had a wonderful time. *Conversation coach.* That is one profession that would not suit my mother. At every meal, she makes sure all the guests have everything they need, but she never takes part in the discussion. If I think about it, I realize that I don't even know what she thinks about most things. For all I know, she might vote far left now. I can't help but restrain a smile, and she raises her eyebrows. She's waiting for me to divulge the reason for my good mood. I'll embroider. I know how to be charming. I am charming. Thoughtful. Polite. The waiter arrives with my double espresso. I really need that coffee this morning.

"Why are you smiling?"

"No reason, Maman. I just wonder how long it's been since the two of us went to a café together."

"Since never, I think. We already didn't go very often when you children were little, and then whenever we did, your sister was with us."

"Is she doing okay?"

"Justine? Oh, yes. Didn't your father tell you, she'll probably be coming for lunch? He would rather she came this evening for *the* family reunion before the big departure, but apparently she has something else planned."

I break into a grin. My sister. A gem. We have been cordially avoiding each other for years. We don't have the same interests. That's the sentence we serve up to everyone who's surprised how little we see of each other. As a rule we add something like, "So it goes! Just because you're siblings it doesn't mean you have to be close." And whoever is listening murmurs in agreement. We're not a big family of siblings. It's just the two of us.

"You know, I may be going away, but the earth will keep on turning. There's no need to go to a lot of bother!"

"It's odd. I thought you'd be staying in Paris."

"Yes, so did I, for a while. But it must be one of the

consequences of the lockdown. I need space. I need the whole planet."

I let out a laugh that rings hollow, even to my ears, and the young woman who's in the back room looks up. I'm loud. One of my characteristics. People are often surprised: my parents are so quiet. My mother often reminds us of the fact that some of her ancestors were from the southwest. That's the archetype I belong to. Boastful. Loud laughter. Well-watered parties in Bayonne. Rugby—yet I've never liked team sports. I have the sort of personality that unsettles people. I'm aware of it. And at the same time, I don't give a damn what others might think about me. After all, I haven't done too badly, thus far.

"So Annabelle won't be going with you, then."

I let out a sigh. I'm instantly sorry, because my mother puts on her pinched look, but I don't feel like elaborating. I'm surprised she actually stoops to come out with a mea culpa, something that really isn't like her:

"I'm sorry, it's none of my business. I suppose it's another consequence of the lockdown. I liked Annabelle, but a mother mustn't go getting attached to her son's conquests. It's a stupid mistake."

"Maman, I—"

"No, drop it. In fact, I don't really feel like discussing all that again, just a few hours before you leave for Canada."

Her gaze lingers on the tables, the bar, the man who has just come in and who, from across the room, is waving to the man waiting by the picture window. His face reminds me of someone, but who? Maman is holding forth. She says how pretty this place is, that it's all new, or nearly. She supposes the owners must have used the time during lockdown to redecorate. I stifle a yawn. I didn't sleep well. The atmosphere at my parents' place is oppressive. Maman has gone off on a tangent now. This time it's the turn of the banquettes. Apparently they're *the* ultimate mark of poor taste. The leatherette upholstery, absolutely horrible. And so uncomfortable! It's incredible the owners haven't realized.

Suddenly, somewhere in the middle of a sentence, Lucie.

I listen more carefully. According to my father, Lucie is the source of the danger. No, of course not. Maman glosses over it. She's explaining that this place reminds her of her childhood. Every Sunday morning she went with Grandpa to the swimming pool. Afterward, he always took her to the same café for a mint soda, a place run by a tall redheaded woman.

"For a long time I wondered if they were sleeping together."

I put my cup back down a bit too hastily. Brown liquid splashed onto the dark green saucer. My father is right. Her behavior has changed. My real mother would never have gossiped, or used an expression like "sleep together." I hesitate over how to answer, but she continues her soliloquy, and while she's speaking it's as if she were spreading her wings. She sits up straight, ventures to place her right arm on the back of the banquette, even allows herself a little half smile.

"I went back to that café once when I was a teenager, but it was completely changed. There was no sign of that tall redheaded woman, or of the two dull-witted waiters she used to order around. When you're a child, you think the world will never budge, and then you grow up and one day you find yourself in a place that has nothing to do anymore with the image you'd kept in your mind. Lucie says that's the way things should be, because there's nothing worse than the failure to act. Personally, I'm more reserved. I would have liked to freeze time, back when you were ten and your sister seven. Everything was fine then. I'd found my place."

"Who's Lucie?"

"A friend."

She stares at me as she says this, and lets out a short spurt of laughter.

"If you could see your face! Yes, I do actually have friends, you know! Okay, I probably wasn't very sociable when you were little, but that was because it was your father who organized our parties. He's the one who decided who came to dinner and even what the topics of conversation would be. I was relegated—though your father would surely use the word 'promoted'—to the rank of organizer-in-chief. Let's be fair. Never once did he forget to congratulate me and to brag during dinner about what a perfect wife he had. I thought it was a strange expression, but I didn't protest. That was not my role. And besides, the meals were so overwhelming! I always ended up with the most horrible headaches, but of course I didn't tell anyone, because your father was already snoring by the time I got to bed, and the next morning I was, naturally, the first one up. Listen, Guillaume, please, close your mouth, you look like a cleaner fish against the glass of an aquarium in an Asian restaurant."

I blush. I can feel it spreading across my shoulders, up my neck. I'm stunned. I think that's the first time this has ever happened. I've just been told off by the woman who brought me into this world. It takes me a few seconds to regain my composure.

"That doesn't exactly tell me who this Lucie is."

My mother frowns then stares at me with something brazen in her gaze. Detaching each syllable, she replies that Lucie's an old classmate from the lycée who's opened a book store on rue Montgolfier. She sits back an inch or two and says, "Well! Are you acting under orders, by any chance?"

Once again I feel the heat spreading through my skin. It's very unsettling. My voice catches as I try to say "Sorry?" and that convinces no one. In any case not the woman across from me, who looks away and shakes her head. I hunt in vain for the right response and I'm annoyed that I didn't antici pate her reaction. It's not like me. But deep down, it's not like me, either, to agree to help my father; he asked me to use the time I'd be spending with my mother to put out feelers and try to figure out what was going on in her mind. She's right about one thing: children shouldn't get involved in their par ents' lives, and vice versa, once they no longer live under the same roof. She takes a sip of tea, makes a face, and carries on. This is getting more and more embarrassing.

"What I think, is that your father's afraid I've become a lesbian, which, given the state of our sexual relations, would genuinely make me happy. He's not afraid I don't love him anymore, he really doesn't give a damn, and he must be finding ways to make up for it elsewhere. No. What he dreads more than anything is what other people might say."

She's raised her voice slightly. I'm not sure she realizes. At the same time, the waiter has turned down the volume on the music. I got the impression everyone heard what my mother just said. That young woman at the back, in any case, is all ears. If it were up to me, I'd give her the finger. But I have manners. I get it from my father—and my mother, until today. So all I do is clear my throat. My mother pays no attention. She keeps unwinding the yarn of her story. Now that she's free to speak, there's no stopping her.

"Listen, Guillaume, I'm going to help you. I'll give you all the details you need for your investigation. If you need to take notes, I have a pen and a notebook in my bag. Unless you'd rather record me, perhaps? You could use it as evidence in court."

I'm really annoyed with myself. I was caught off guard, and now I'm exposed. She can fire her rockets wherever she likes. It's open territory. She goes back to this famous Lucie. She explains that the two of them went to the same secondary school, even though they didn't hang out with the same crowd, of course. Lucie was very popular and got invited to all the parties. A bundle of energy. Irresistible. Never at a loss for words. They really liked it, those boys who were trying to be like their fathers, the way Lucie would put them in their place. Or how she'd kiss them and bite them, *yes, yes, I swear.*

Maman gives a sigh. She says that, in the end, she's never understood men. They should have despised Lucie—her frankness, her freedom—but it was just the opposite. In the beginning, anyway. Having said that, they never envisaged a lasting relationship with her. To share their life, they'd rather pick a girl who was more docile. Someone from the same background.

"Ninnies like me, in other words."

I can't help but smile at her using the word "ninny." My real mother is back. This is so typical of her, this old-fashioned vocabulary. *Ninny.* Does my father think she's a ninny? No, surely not, contrary to what she's insinuating. She intimidates him, I think. And me? Do I look down on her? The question hovers in the air while she takes a sip of tea and closes her eyes. Her body relaxes and her wrinkles fade all of a sudden. She looks ten or twenty years younger. Once again she's the woman I knew when I was a child. It's really striking.

She starts up about Lucie again. She explains that, running into each other at the local library on Saturday afternoons, they'd discovered a mutual passion. Reading. Both of them devoured all the contemporary novels their teachers had never recommended. They explored worlds their classmates had never dreamed of.

"You know, your grandparents went on and on about how incredibly important reading was, but I never saw them pick up a book. And yet they bought them all the time. The current bestsellers. Then they'd position them carefully on the shelves in the living room so that guests would notice them when they came over for an aperitif, but it never went any further. They did, on the other hand, allow me to borrow any of those books. As long as I remained docile and obedient. And didn't forget to go out from time to time with my girlfriends, because in their opinion, don't you know, nothing could beat shopping. That's the way it was. So we read, Lucie and I, and we kept an interested, kindly eye on each other, without going so far as to communicate openly. So when she opened her bookstore, I was one of her first customers. That's all there is to it."

I'm about to add an uncalled-for "Are you sure?", but she cuts me off, reminding me that I've been in the same sort of situation with Annabelle, haven't I? Sometimes, the less you know about your immediate family, the better. We're on the same wavelength. All this business has nothing to do with me. All the more so as I'm leaving tomorrow and will be thousands of miles away from here, and when I get there I'll have to self-isolate for two weeks, even though I'm double-vaccinated. Another chapter is about to begin.

My mother gives a vague smile, as if she was hardly aware of my presence. And yet, when she starts speaking again, it's as if she'd been following the twists and turns of my thoughts.

"I suppose, what with Covid and the health restrictions, I won't see you again for at least six months. Maybe even a year."

"The virus won't last forever. Even with the variants."

"Have you, too, turned into an epidemiologist lately?"

That's three times that my cheeks have blushed bright red. This time, it's downright unpleasant and I don't feel like ducking the issue.

"I stay informed, like everyone. Except that I understand the articles I read. Even the scientific ones. It's my basic training, after all, and you were very proud of my results in physics and biology."

She pats my hand, the way you would pat that of an old man or a sullen child.

"Don't be angry. Let's not spoil our last moments together. You're an adult. You live your life the way you see fit. The main thing is for you to be happy. Because you are happy, aren't you?"

"Absolutely."

"So much the better. Oh, by the way, the famous Lucie who your father is afraid might be my lover told me that you were in middle school together with her daughter, Léa."

"Oh really? Léa what?"

"Longuet."

I let a few seconds go by. I feel my jaws contracting slightly. For a moment I'm afraid that Léa Longuet is about to appear on the other side of the picture window. But she doesn't. That's all ancient history. Outside, it has finally stopped raining.

"Sorry, that doesn't ring a bell. But there were Léas by the cartload, you know. And now, help me, since you detected my arsenal of spyware, what shall I tell Papa? Knowing him, he's already on tenterhooks."

She sighs, takes a sip of tea, but then moans because it's cold, and these tiny teapots, honestly, it's an insult, given the price you pay.

"Tell him I'll be filing for divorce soon. I just hope we'll be able to finalize things in an amicable fashion, particularly now that you and your sister are old enough to look after yourselves, so anyway...We can do without lawyers, don't you think?"

She's thrown me for a loop. She waits for my reaction, not missing a beat.

"Goodness, you really do have a tendency to sit there with your jaw dropped these days. You'd better not behave like that at the company where you'll be working, otherwise they'll think they've hired an imbecile."

I ignore her unkind remark. I'm thinking about my father. About the family. The future. My thoughts are all jostling together. My brain is a battlefield.

"But how will you manage financially?"

"Oh, that...Don't worry. Lucie's apprentice is going to live with her boyfriend in Clermont-Ferrand. She'll hire me. And if that's not enough, I'll dust off my literature degrees. It's funny, in this family no one seems to recall that I went to university and got a master's degree—well, what they called a master's back then. It's probably because literature doesn't count for much around here, does it? In any case, they always need substitute teachers at the Éducation Nationale. And they're not fussy. They don't care how old you are as long as you have a few diplomas and are battle-ready. I'll manage, no problem."

"And . . . the house?"

"What about the house? It's not going to collapse! If your father wants to buy my share and keep it and look after it, he's very welcome. Otherwise, well, we'll sell it. That's what usually happens, isn't it?"

"I don't know. I'm not an expert on divorce."

"For you, honestly, it won't change much. You'll be living thousands of miles away. Your father will go and see you very soon. You've always had so much in common. As for me, you'll come and see me once a year. You'll see how I've blossomed. Okay, it will probably be a bit more complicated for your sister, but she's already aware of the situation, and she approves of what I'm doing."

"I beg your pardon?"

My mother shrugs and flings back that my sister is more attentive than I am, and above all, she can count on Justine being there for her more often. Apparently, she's been aware for a long time of the extent of the damage, and it pains her to see her mother treated with so much indifference.

I cannot believe what I'm hearing. Justine could have kept me up to speed, after all! All of a sudden, here we are in the middle of a trench war, the women on one side and the men on the other, it's unbelievable. I didn't think we were that kind of family.

I don't have time to dwell on this. My mother points out that, since I'm playing errand boy, she's got one for me. She'll leave it up to me to convey her intentions to my father. I shouldn't keep him waiting too long, he's probably getting really impatient to hear what I've found out. As for my mother, she'll sit here in the café a little longer. She's really come to like this place, in the end. She thanks me for bringing her here. From now on, whenever I think of her, she wants me to picture her in this new setting. Other than that, she hasn't prepared anything for lunch, for once. Justine won't mind. We'll snack on whatever we find. Or else we'll get takeout from the new Japanese restaurant. She loves their sushi.

"Unless your father suddenly feels like taking up cooking again. When he was younger, he was very good at it, you know. See you later!"

Dismissed. Like a flunky. I feel the fury rising inside so I rush out before I start screaming. Tomorrow I'll be gone. Tomorrow, all these people—my mother, my father, my sister, Lucie, and Léa Longuet—will no longer exist and will vanish even from my computer screen.

Move to trash.

Empty trash.

FABRICE, 31—BAR STOOL NUMBER 1

I WIPE MY GLASSES with the sleeve of my sodden jacket, to little effect. I'm mad at myself, because on the radio this morning they even said there'd be storms, and I swore I'd take my raincoat or a jacket with a hood, but of course when it was time to leave, I forgot. I headed out on foot with a ton of stuff on my mind, and before I even had time to realize, I was soaked through to the bone. When I came into the bar, José looked at me disapprovingly—sometimes I wonder who's the boss and who's the employee around here. It's probably because we don't fit any of those stubborn stereotypes. José is the same age as I am, but we've known each other for so long that over the years he's become my father, my mother, my brother, my uncle, my sovereign, and my vassal all rolled into one. He tossed me a towel from behind the bar and murmured, "Your hair!," motioned with his chin to the stool we call "number one," and without my asking, fixed me a double espresso. I don't know what I'd do without him. For a start, I wouldn't open this early. I took a sip of coffee, thanked him, and asked about the Covid pass. He shrugged and said that they hadn't decided anything yet. He said that in England, despite the dramatic rise in the number of cases, the pubs were still open. We both smiled. Neither one of us has much respect for Boris Johnson. Even less for Trump and Bolsonaro, obviously. On the things that matter, the two of us see eye to eye. He added that we could see how the situation evolved, on a day-to-day basis. We've done pretty well so far, haven't we?

I glanced around the room. For a Thursday morning with horrible weather, it actually wasn't too bad. There's the girl at the back—the one who's been coming every day since we reopened, and who stays there until evening. One man who came in just before I did and joined his friend at table number two. A mother and her son, table three—and just as I was looking at them, the son leapt to his feet, nearly knocking over his cup, and rushed out. The mother smiled and rolled her eyes. She waved to José, but I went over to her. She had a complaint, she said, with a smile. This teapot, really, it's very meager. Honestly, when you order a cup of tea, you take the time that goes with it. You let it steep, you idle away the minutes a little, you drink the first cup, and then a second one—anyway, you can see what I'm getting at. She was prepared to pay a lot more, she insisted, but only for a genuinely relaxing experience—and God knows she needs one. I nodded and gave it some thought. Yes, we should have something that would do the trick. Yes, she was right. Even if we weren't, strictly speaking, a tearoom, we must provide our customers with the best. I went back behind the bar and José muttered, "What does she want?" in that voice that's more adept at getting rid of tipsy customers than attracting the middle-aged morning crowd. I told him not to worry about it. I'd deal with it. I can play the ideal son-in-law, although I'm neither a son-in-law nor ideal, but it goes down really well with that particular type of clientele. From under the bar counter I dug out a heavy porcelain teapot whose very existence José knew nothing about. I washed it with great care, brought the water to the boil, and carried it out with the box full of teabags. The customer was thrilled. I could sense, behind my back, how annoyed José was. At times there are details he fails to take into account. Like the presence of that young woman at the table in the back, the one I call the artist and whom he insists on calling the scribbler. She pisses him off. Not me. She's a cat in a living room. She curls up in her corner. She inhabits the place, and the place definitely needs to be inhabited, after a year and a half of orders and counter-orders, of closures, of reopening with QR codes on the menus and masks to be worn, then curfews. I don't know how it is we're still standing. Like the healthcare workers, I suppose: because we have no other choice.

These walls belong to me. I bought them two years ago. Jocelyne was tired. She was looking for a buyer and she refused to sell her café to the Lebrun sons, who already own half the cafés in town, and who are playing Monopoly with all the businesses. Jocelyne was in no hurry. She was sixty-eight, and ready to retire, but not at any cost. Jocelyne insists on the fact that she's always been a free woman—hardheaded, some would say. A very strong-willed woman—that's what they used to call those women warriors, just after the world wars were over. They never married. Love affairs from time to time, but not with anyone in the same trade—no mixing business with emotions, even when they hadn't grown attached. She hadn't been destined for that career. Her parents wanted her to become a doctor. Or a nurse. A profession in healthcare, so in their old age they could have ready access, or so they thought, to informed advice. They needn't have worried. In July 1976, on the national highway number ten, a truck blocked both the road and their hopes of a future, for all eternity.

Jocelyne was twenty-three at the time, working at the local pharmacy while she waited to retake the healthcare exams she couldn't seem to pass. She inherited a little house that she immediately put on the market. She made a few wise investments. Ever since she was little she'd been fascinated by the stock exchange, by stocks and bonds, and she knew exactly which sector she wanted to invest in. The future would be read in computers. A lot was at stake, but she knew that if she lost her money, no one would come and criticize her for it. That was real freedom. In a few years she managed to amass a fair amount of money.

She quit her job. She got hired as a waitress by some friends of her parents, who before long gave her greater responsibilities, once they realized that Jocelyne knew what she was doing, whether it came to accounting and managing inventory or handling rude clients. She was never at a loss for words, and knew how to command respect. "I'm a bulldozer. I knock down every wall," she says, when she's had too much to drink, which doesn't happen often, because

Jocelyne hates losing control, hates not so much speaking out of turn as expressing herself too clearly. She doesn't have much faith in humankind, which keeps her from being disappointed, she says.

She has faith in me. She's right. She's often told me that she would have liked to have a son like me. I don't know what to say. I just look her right in the eye. She looks away and says that if the café doesn't work out, I can easily find a job as a gigolo. And specifies that she could set herself up as a madam in her old age. She'll have no trouble finding female clients for me. Or male ones. As I please.

Jocelyne had her heart set on a café located just across the street from the Lycée des Terrasses. The Atlantic. Back then, it was a seedy dump that attracted only local winos, its reputation tainted by a number of brawls and even an alleged murder. When the owner decided to throw in the towel, Jocelyne bought the place for a song. She brought in teams of skilled laborers and ordered them around with insolence and an iron hand, while fixing them irresistible meals—they didn't go home at midday anymore, they stayed there and were even more productive for it. They knocked down walls, filled in cracks, carried out tons of rubble, put in huge picture windows, repainted the walls. All in record time. Jocelyne had invested everything she'd made from her dabbling in the stock market into this project, and the general opinion was that she'd gone crazy. So they didn't believe in her? She methodically crossed their names off in her little address book.

She'd noticed the students from the lycée, how aimless they seemed when they ambled down the dead-end street that led to the school. They spent their money at the bakery. They hung around in groups, laughing loudly, occupying the bus shelters when it began to rain, going around in circles, sometimes fighting. She would draw them to her café—it would be their first café, the one they'd reminisce about decades later with tears in their eyes. She would listen to them rejoicing and complaining. She would play the part of confidante. She knew times had changed, that teenagers had pocket money and an urge to spend. They simply didn't have a place to congregate. She was going to give them one.

That was exactly what happened. Jocelyne started by putting up a poster that read, "change of ownership," followed by a second one, "students welcome." It didn't take more than a week for her first customers to venture in. Word of mouth did the rest to perfection, attracting students from other lycées in town, too, and in the evening, a few older ones from the Technical Institute that had just opened. But they didn't stay for long when they found out that Jocelyne didn't intend to keep the place open past eight p.m. She smiled and explained that she, too, had a family life, and that she had to get up early. School started at eight o'clock, the café opened forty-five minutes before that.

A family life. Under no circumstance did Jocelyne want a family life. What she needed, when she got back to her apartment, was peace and quiet. After days spent watching her young customers falling in love, swapping insults or jumping to the rescue, tearing themselves apart, lending support, and pledging eternal friendship (which would last only a few months), she felt satiated and exhausted. Her solitude no longer weighed on her. She was still young, but not young enough to go to a discothèque without looking out of place. She didn't feel like hanging out in other bars once night had fallen. She gradually cut herself off from other people.

One day while smoking one of her famous long menthol cigarettes, she told me that her life had somehow been diluted by the adolescents'. And as they grew, they went off to pursue their college education in other towns, migrating to the capital without planning to return; they would be replaced by others, just as annoying and endearing, raucous and tender. She learned new first names, heard new music, discovered new idols. Time seemed endless. Her only disappointment, basically, was that those students who'd hung around for hours in her café very rarely came back to see her once they'd left the neighborhood. She was part of a scene they eventually filed away in some recess of their memory. One day they'd remember the café existed, and they'd try to recall the owner's name: *Sure you do, you know, the blond woman with her never-ending cigarettes, come on, what was her name?!*

I was one of the few who remained loyal.

I think loyalty is one of my best features, maybe the most important one. Along with sentimentality. Most people I talk with view that as a failing. As if attachment to others were a form of weakness, particularly when you're not related "by blood." You should focus only on those who are "truly close"—your nuclear family, your parents, children; as for anyone else, enough! Friends of mine often put forth this argument, and I reply that if that's the case, I should ignore them. They laugh, and retort that they are part of my extended family, in fact, that they're like brothers to me, or cousins. I nod. I act as if I understand. I know that as soon as they turn away, I'll be once again the last thing on their minds. Being sentimental has never implied a lack of lucidity. I know very well who the pillars of my existence are. Jocelyne. José. And I've known it for years. They're the crutches that have allowed me to make my way. I'm still wobbly, but I'm gaining in confidence and self-assurance.

I've always been touched by the stories people tell me—and they tell me a lot of them. I'm not the kind of guy people fall madly in love with—my nose is straight but a little short, I'm too thin, my beard hides part of my face, and my right eye seems slightly bigger than the left one. I appear fragile. That's probably why the people I speak with feel like sharing some of their load with me. They figure I'm not going to hurt them. That I'm a bird. That their worries will slide over my feathers and then I'll be able to take them elsewhere, far away. By the time they leave, they feel a sense of relief. They thank me. They feel sorry for me, too. They wonder what will become of me. In their opinion, being a repository is not an up-and-coming profession. They're wrong.

I understood very early on how powerful the ability to listen can be. To listen and then act, with the utmost discretion. It began with José. Then with those girls who asked themselves questions, and came to the conclusion that maybe I was the answer, even if it was only temporary. And finally, with Jocelyne.

We were here, in this café, which was already called Le Tom's, since she was the one who'd given it that strange name. She had just informed us that she was going to retire soon. The Atlantic had gone downhill after a few prosperous years, because the students wanted to be farther away from school, and they started spending their time in bars and cafés in the town center, where they paid top dollar for elaborate cocktails with exotic names. Jocelyne herself was no longer as attached to her café as she'd once been, ever since she'd had a disappointment in love. She sold the premises to the bank branch next door, which was seeking to expand. She'd gotten a good price. She'd hesitated—should she get a new start somewhere else, or retire from the business and invest in the stock market, since she'd done so well all those years ago. The 2008 financial crisis left her more cautious. She started looking for a new spot. She found this café that doubled as a betting shop. She knew the owner. He warned her that it was risky for a woman on her own. She answered back: she'd know how to surround herself with the right people, and what was more, she'd stop selling cigarettes and lottery tickets. She'd also get rid of the Formica tables and the chairs with wicker seats. The place had potential, and she'd put it to good use. The owner burst out laughing and gave her a solid thump on the back. He warned her that there was every likelihood it wouldn't even get off the ground. She shrugged. She'd seen worse.

They were neither right nor wrong. The bar was redecorated a bit too hastily, and it effectively put off the former clientele, without really attracting a new one. People would stop in, but there were not many regulars, and Jocelyne made just enough to pay herself and her sole employee—an intimidating hulk called Tony—the minimum wage. They stuck it out for nearly ten years, but when Tony finally jumped ship, Jocelyne decided to retire.

I was stunned. This café had become my hideout and my anchor—just as The Atlantic had, during my adolescence. When I went into Le Tom's for the first time, Jocelyne immediately recognized me and greeted me with a broad smile. She was always pleased when she got news of her "alumni."

It wasn't the most glorious time of my life. I'd studied computer networks but I soon realized that I was bored out of my mind by the jobs I was offered. I was vegetating. Emotionally, I had become a sort of serial monogamist. I had relationships which lasted six months or a year, and then after a while, the girls lost interest or found something better elsewhere. They held no grudges against me, or very few. They simply criticized my temperament as being so even that it seemed like nothing ever fazed me. I showed no ambition. I was slowly rotting away in uninteresting jobs. I watched all the TV series everyone was talking about without displaying the slightest emotion. My most recent fiancée, Anaïs, who was a nurse, blew up one evening—did I even notice the tragedies of the planet, like the extreme temperatures, the probable end of humanity? Or the political scandals? The

inequality between men and women? The #MeToo movement? I couldn't get a word in edgewise. She decreed that I
must, in fact, have been suffering from depression for a long
time already, since it was one of those diseases that lay hidden
for years and wore your organism down until nothing seemed
to make any difference. She made me promise to see a doctor.
I hadn't started looking yet, and then Jocelyne told me about
her plans. I was determined to give it a shot—because deep
down even I found myself pretty strange. Apart from José I
didn't really have any friends. I could even delete the word
"really." I had no friends, even though I was convinced that
people who met me thought I was a likeable enough guy.

When Jocelyne told us that she was going to bow out,
the others pretended not to believe her. I merely stared at
her, while she was busy behind the bar. She thought she'd
spend part of her retirement here—from October to April,
roughly, because she had a house with a little garden that she
loved; and the rest of the year in a little apartment on the
coast of the Atlantic, which remained to be found. So this
year she was going to close the café, over the next two weeks
(doleful protests from the regulars), to find the right place.
The problem, she added that evening, was that she wasn't
a very good driver, and age wasn't helping any. What was
more, two weeks of schlepping around real estate agencies in
seaside resorts that were still half deserted at this time of year
was enough to destroy your morale. So, she was looking for
someone to go with her. She'd already asked her friends, but
none of them were tempted by her proposal. And naturally

they all had appointments with their specialists, implant therapists, cardiologists, and osteopaths. In short, they were falling apart. Would this trip interest anyone among the present company, by any chance? She couldn't offer any sort of compensation—that would be pushing it—but she would, of course, cover all expenses.

I raised my hand, like in elementary school. The other customers couldn't believe it. For once I was showing an interest in something. Jocelyne smiled and murmured, "Fabrice, I knew it." She gave me a high-five. We would leave in two days' time. Now bring out the champagne. On the house.

All those people you see off and on for years, and you never have any idea of how important they can turn out to be in your life. José. Jocelyne. During that strange week we spent, the two of us, looking for the hidden gem that would be her summer home, I opened up to Jocelyne, far more than to anyone, ever. The fact that The Atlantic had been a refuge for me just when things at home were getting really tense—my father screaming at my mother, calling her every name in the book; the suburban neighborhood where we lived; the neighbors, witnessing arguments and the increasing alcoholism of both husband and wife. The certainty, in the housing development, this would all end badly. At The Atlantic—on the overcrowded wooden benches, in the middle of all the laughter and commotion, between the foosball table, the pinball machine, and the ancient jukebox, where some of the records would never change because Jocelyne loved them more than anything—everything seemed simple.

I was almost popular. People slapped me on the shoulder, spoke to me about the future, what it had in store for us, the careers we'd pursue. I let myself be lulled by it all. It gave me an impression of belonging somewhere. When it eventually closed—even though by then I was going less and less often—it was truly wrenching.

On the Atlantic coast, the real estate agents took us for mother and son, and we didn't bother setting them straight. We slipped easily into our roles. Sometimes we even overacted. She would come out with things like, "Honestly, can you imagine me living here, son?" We were frequently offered adjacent rooms. It was early June. The season had begun but the restaurants were still empty. When they found out that Jocelyne was in the business, the proprietors would offer us a glass of liqueur with our coffee, and never failed to bring up a golden age which was simply that of their own youth. They gave us advice, too, deriding the real estate agencies we were using, scribbling on a scrap of paper the contact information for people who were "much more reliable."

In the end, she set her heart on Arcachon in southwestern France, reasoning that the Bay of Biscay would be an ideal refuge. She no longer had the youth or the sturdy bones to swim into the breakers head-on. And besides, there was the promenade along the waterfront. There were boats for trips to the Île aux Oiseaux. An authentic small town with all the shops nearby. I pointed out that the prices were exorbitant, and property was hard to find, but she shrugged. She had faith. She was right to. We found an apartment in a quiet building some distance from the livelier district. Three rooms, recently repainted, quite obviously overpriced, but Jocelyne paid the full asking price in cash. Out on the tiny balcony she murmured, "It will be perfect here."

She insisted on taking me out to dinner at one of those luxury hotels where our casual attire looked out of place. As the waiter was leading us toward the back of the room, she headed for a table by the rounded window, signaling to the young man that we were probably rich enough to buy the place and so he could stop treating us like peasants, thank you very much. She ordered a bottle of champagne and a huge platter of shellfish for two. I had to confess that I had no idea how to shell crayfish or crabs—no one had ever taught me the technique. First time for everything, she said. For shelling shellfish, for running a café. The waiter brought the bottle. We raised our glasses. The week that was coming to an end would change for good not only her life, but mine as well. She had decided, before even coming out with her invitation back at Le Tom's that evening, that whoever took up her offer to share the journey, if they proved themselves worthy, she would make them her sole heir. I frowned, and after a few seconds I said that we weren't in an Agatha Christie novel, that I was pretty sure that in France the law was far more complicated than that. Lawmakers had come up with safeguards to prevent old ladies from being ill-used by gigolos like me. She burst out laughing, and the headwaiter rolled his eyes. Dear Lord. A social climber, no doubt. One who had recently won the lottery. They were the worst.

"Don't you worry about me. I've been spending plenty of time in lawyers' and notaries' offices these last few months. I made my fortune all by myself. I have no descendants and no extended family, and if I can't stop the State from taking the share it is owed, I can at least keep a good chunk from them. I won't last forever. I will be making my arrangements. The apartment I chose with you will also be yours."

"And if I refuse?"

"You would be a fool."

"It wouldn't be the first time."

"I know. But you'll take the time to think it over and you will agree. Because you're bound to give in to the will of a fragile little thing like me. Tell me, you're not working at the moment, are you?"

"No. That's why I can play chauffeur."

"Then what I suggest is that you start by taking over the café."

"I do what?"

"Le Tom's. I don't have the energy or the required gift of the gab anymore. The Lebrun sons have their eye on the place. They're already in the running. The problem is that I don't like them. They've been chomping at the bit for so long, wanting to buy this place, that they've worn their teeth down to stumps."

"You'd rather have someone who knows nothing about it."

She took a sip of champagne, then said, serenely, looking out at the deserted waterfront, "I was so happy when you raised your hand. You've always been one of my favorites, from The Atlantic days. And what's more, you've stayed loyal. You stopped by to say hello from time to time. It's rare, loyalty. It's a quality that must be cherished. So, I cherish you."

It was there, in that setting where we looked so out of place, that she spelled out the details of the entire business. She would take care of the legal aspects. At first, I would be there as a manager and partner, until I got used to the work, particularly the administrative side. Not to worry, she'd let me in on some of the tricks of the trade which, she said, would have saved her a lot of time if someone had explained them to her right from the start, and in any case, we'd have accountants to help us. Then, soon after, she'd finalize her will. She'd already gone into things very thoroughly. A series of charitable donations. The absolutely staggering amount she would still owe the State, since there was no way around it. Obviously it would have been simpler if she'd had children, but there was no point dwelling on something that hadn't happened. I held up my hand to interrupt.

"In short, I'm becoming your son."

"You already have parents."

I thought about them. About the strange life they were leading now. Back in the days when I went to The Atlantic, I was convinced that their divorce was inevitable, and I prayed for it with all my might, I was that fed up with their bickering and abuse. And then my father had his first stroke, followed by a second one a few months later. He became much calmer, changed his diet, above all quit the alcohol and cigarettes. He had retired not long before. He went for long walks—hikes that took him to the edge of town. My mother stopped worrying about him. She'd had it up to here. She spent her days doing exactly as she pleased. She'd decided to go on working, although she was over sixty-two. She insisted it wasn't for the money, even if it was a considerable sum. It was for the social side. For the friends she had at work. My parents crossed paths with each other in the rooms of their house, which was beginning to show signs of wear—they'd have to deal with the window insulation soon. They were cordial with each other. They were housemates. Even they couldn't get over it, how quiet the house was now. They'd also decided, once and for all, not to worry about me anymore, about my love life or my professional future. I was obviously a failure, particularly when you saw how successful the neighbors' children were, but what could they do? They'd given me every chance, and if I hadn't seized a single one of them, that was my problem, not theirs. I was over thirty years old. We all have our cross to bear.

Jocelyne finished her glass of champagne. She added that this filiation business was purely symbolic. We didn't owe each other anything. She would never ask me to look after her when she got too old and helpless. She would simply inform me when the time came to go with her to the clinic in Switzerland specialized in gentle leave-takings.

"Right, let's not end on such a grotesque note. Let's talk about you, rather."

"About me? But there's nothing to say."

"Your love life."

"A complete desert. Not even sure there's an oasis on the horizon."

"Have you tried dating sites?"

I sighed. Nowadays when you reach your thirties, people constantly ask you that. No, I haven't joined the vast community of singles looking for affairs or perfect love in the international catalogue of programmed encounters. Yes, it's probably a mistake. Misplaced pride. The idiotic impression that when you're reduced to looking on the Internet for something you didn't manage to find in your everyday life, it means you're really maladjusted. Across from me Jocelyne merely smiled. There was a trace of lipstick on one of her upper teeth.

"I won't hold it against you. That's not my role and above all, it's none of my business. But I've kept my eye on you all these years."

"Sorry?"

"At The Atlantic, for a start. I remember you were in love with this girl . . . What was her name? The one who dressed like a tramp but was rolling in dough? Élise something or other, wasn't it?"

"Élise Legrand. I can't believe it! You remember Élise Legrand?"

"With that way she had of tossing her long blond hair back when she laughed. A real caricature. Her filthy sneakers that she liked to prop on my banquettes, so I had to tell her every time to get them off of there."

It was my turn to smile. Élise Legrand and her tousled hair, when all her classmates spent hours with their straightening irons. The quilted jackets she bought at Oxfam in London. A caricature of flea-market alternative globalization.

"Did you know that her parents used to run the biggest cardboard manufacturer in Europe?"

"I found out later, yes."

"You had a real thing about her, didn't you?"

I gave a faint sign of acknowledgment, looking away, because I felt the wave washing over me. It was ridiculous. So much water under the bridge. Jocelyne touched my arm.

"She took you for a ride. It happens. That's the age when you're testing your powers of seduction. You and her both. It's pointless. But I felt bad for you, you see. I saw how it was eating away at you, and I knew there was no hope. Did you ever hear what became of her, later on?"

"Indirectly. She went to Paris. To study law, I think. She wanted to get into Sciences Po . . . Anyway."

"And since then?"

I shrugged. I muttered that the conversation was getting awkward. Jocelyne burst out laughing. She said that was normal—she knew she could be very awkward. I heard myself say that I'd had casual relationships here and there, nothing conclusive, nothing that lasted very long, either. Girls expected me to have more substance. Or ambition. Or stature, in other words.

"If it's stature they want, they can have it on a platter."

I wanted to say something ironic but didn't, because basically, she was right.

"I have one last question."

"Go ahead."

"Why is the café called Le Tom's?"

"Waiter! May we have the bill, please? We're going to have to move along. And to be honest, the meal wasn't bad but nothing to write home about. So watch out. I never post anything on social media, but this young man sitting across from me is the supreme expert at passing judgment and delivering criticism."

The waiter blushed bright crimson. Jocelyne leaned over to me. She simply murmured, "I'll tell you later," and made me promise not to change the name of the café. Ever. Even when she was dead and buried. I promised.

That's it. That's how my life was turned upside down. With a snap of the fingers, I became someone else. A man who accepts his responsibilities and who plans for the months ahead. A man who constantly keeps an eye on expenses and income. A man who hires people and handles conflicts with the clientele. The first employee I hired was José, of course. It couldn't have been any other way. And Jocelyne has kept her word—she's given me a free hand.

And yet there are still a few traces of the man I once was. Heartburn waking me up at night sometimes. The way I bow my head when I walk past some of the posh houses on Avenue Parmentier, because I know that I'll never belong to that world, and I still haven't learned to be proud of my roots.

And then there's the way I hesitate, so annoyingly, every time I come into this café that belongs to me now. My walls. My possession. My property.

Everybody says it's a funny name for a French café. With the apostrophe and Anglo-Saxon "s" that don't belong to our grammar or culture. We've already got enough English in shop signs and fast-food chains. What's more, there's something a little old-fashioned about it, isn't there? You picture the interior: it will have deep brown and orange armchairs, low hanging lamps, and heavily made-up women talking to men in wide striped neckties. A shady meeting place straight out of the 1970s. I let people come up with their theories. Sooner or later, someone always asks me why I chose such a name.

I reply that I didn't choose anything at all, because it was the former owner who named the place. She made me promise not to change it. Customers raise their eyebrows. They snicker and say, "And you went along with that?" I smile. I tell them that I keep my promises, that's all. And besides, it's actually quite appropriate, since one of my middle names is Thomas. It's a sort of wink. A passing of the baton. The customer nods. That makes sense. They're glad I've shared this with them. They'll repeat the anecdote from time to time. It's proof they know the owner and that it's a sort of a home away from home.

My name is actually Fabrice Michel Joseph Ortega. No one would ever have dreamed of calling me Thomas. My father had Spanish origins but he wanted his offspring to be viewed right away as pure French stock. The Miguel of my ancestors morphed quite naturally into Michel. The Josepha who had raised my mother lost the last letter of her name when she came to figure on my ID card. Fabrice? When I asked my mother and father they couldn't remember exactly how they came up with it. It was a trendy name. There was a famous radio presenter called Fabrice; singers, too.

My name is Fabrice Michel Joseph Ortega, but now, for a lot of locals, I've become "the owner of Le Tom's." I'm sure someday I'll be known as Tom, period. I won't mind. It will be poetic justice.

I glance around the room. There are a few people after all. Every morning I come in with a knot in my stomach. What if the café stays empty all day long? And no one feels like coming here, what with the health restrictions, the masks and all the rest, for so long now? I wonder how many of the regulars have been vaccinated. Personally, I don't have a problem with it. I got the jab as soon as I could. I figured we'd never see the end of it, otherwise. I was surprised when José followed suit. I thought he'd be more reluctant. Ifemelu assured me she'd had her shot, too, but she's never brought me any proof, and I haven't asked her for any.

It's stopped raining. I'm wondering if I should set up the terrace—it'll be exhausting if I suddenly have to take everything inside again in a mad rush—but I think I should. The terrace is where everyone congregates. Particularly at Le Tom's. It gives onto a little square with a fountain, a few benches, and a scattering of trees for shade when there's a heat wave—which we won't get this summer. José nods in the direction of the young woman at the table in the back and gives a nasty snort.

"I'm sure she comes here because of you."

"Or you, José. Don't underestimate your sex appeal."

"Would I ever. Anyway, in the meantime, we could suggest she order something more to drink, don't you think?"

"She's not bothering anyone, José. We'll see, later. But if you want, I'll clear her table."

I notice his faint smile. He's relieved. I don't know what she did to make him despise her so. Maybe he's afraid she'll sketch him and the portrait won't be flattering. That would be a pity. José is worth a lot more than he allows himself to show. Obviously, I'm biased. But I'm probably also the person who knows him best. I wonder why the guy at table three went out in such a rush, just now. His mother is lingering over her second cup of tea. What could she be thinking about? Her son's sudden desertion? The day ahead of her that's just begun? If I could be granted one particular talent, I'd like to be able to access people's minds and read their most private thoughts. I'm not as discreet as some might think.

10:30 A.M.

FRANÇOISE, 60—TABLE NO. 3

HE LEFT at least half an hour ago, and it's as if I can still hear him speaking. One thing's for sure, he learned how to talk at that prestigious business school we sent him to that cost an arm and a leg. He knows how to alternate between advice, irony, kindness, threats, and reproach; it's impressive. He gets it from his father, but his father isn't as subtle. In the middle of a well-crafted sentence he'll slip in a vulgar word, and it spoils the effect, or he'll make mistakes with his conjugations that the guests pick up on, mentally. Nor does my husband manage to remain impassive—his face changes color, pink, orangish, golden yellow, scarlet, it's often pretty unattractive but sometimes it can be endearing. You think to yourself, he's still got his flaws. Emotions. Something human. With Guillaume, no. Guillaume has fairly matte skin and it hardly ever changes. I'm surprised and honored that, three times in a row, he could not hide his emotion. I can't remember the last time I saw him redden for any other reason than sunburn.

I take another sip of tea. In the end, I feel good here. Awhile ago, when Guillaume literally shoved me inside, I didn't feel comfortable. And then when he called the waiter,

I felt a tension in my shoulders. He was in his element. He was behaving as if he owned the place. I knew instantly that his father had sent him. I suspected as much, anyway. My husband is incapable of speaking to me directly. Our children have become something like telegraph boys at a time when everyone else on the planet is sending tons of text messages and videos.

I think maybe I intimidate Marc now. Once again he can see the woman he was briefly in love with, and whose relative coldness paralyzed him. He didn't understand that beneath my impassive air, I was seething. I dreamed of reading all the books in the library, but also of traveling to every country on earth, and practicing every profession, rising to every challenge. My parents had agreed to let me study modern literature—a remnant of a nineteenth-century education when girls devoted themselves to literature or languages, while waiting to find the right husband.

The right husband came along. He had a strong presence, and that rather overconfident side you often pick up at business school. A mixture of fear regarding what I represented—the old-fashioned bourgeoisie, in which he hoped to thrive—and a desire to make an impact, which wasn't altogether unpleasant. He pretended to be interested in what I was reading, but he never opened a book. On the other hand he did insist on going to museums and memorizing the names of the most famous paintings. I found him endearing, and more sensitive in private than I would have thought. In short, I wouldn't say I'd been trapped. I didn't feel like marriage was something I was just putting up with, at least not initially. Nor did I feel I was just putting up with my pregnancies, or the raising of my children. On the contrary, I was leading a fulfilling life that everyone was comfortable with. *Deep down we've always known that Françoise was born to be a mother. Even that vague desire she had to teach at one point—it was really only that she wanted to be surrounded by children. It's so natural for a woman.* I got so caught up in it all that at one point, it almost made me forget about Lucie.

No. That's not right. She was one of the first people I tried to contact when social media took over, ten years or so ago. Everyone made fun of me because there I was, nearly fifty years old, and I suddenly wanted to know all about the online world. It was my daughter, Justine, who got me started. She'd figured out that I often felt lonely, now that she and her brother didn't seek my company so often anymore. She probably thought, too, that I couldn't reasonably find fault with her for being constantly glued to the screen of her cellphone.

Lucie took years to reply to my friendship request—what a strange combination of terms, when you think about it—I could easily see why. We'd never been close. Maybe she didn't even remember my name. She was busy with other things. Now I know that wasn't the reason why.

In the end she gave in only when I began to visit the bookstore she'd just opened a short distance from the center of town. I'd heard about the new place and I wanted to be one of her first customers. I wanted to support local businesses, something that made Marc and Guillaume sneer in mockery, because for them the only business model is Jeff Bezos. Guillaume even burst out laughing when he found out that Lucie's shop was called Lost Time, and then he apologized and added, "No, really, Maman, honestly, what is that supposed to . . . " I smiled and said, "Proust, maybe?" And we took it no further. Guillaume will surely be my greatest source of regret. He's not the son I'd dreamed of. That's a hard thing to say, but it's nothing compared to his own heartlessness. I take my share of the blame, of course. The other share belongs to my husband, and I'll be leaving him today. He thinks his son is a success; I think he's an absolute failure. Our differences are irreconcilable.

When I went up to speak to Lucie in the shop, after all those years, my voice trembled. It was ridiculous. I asked if she could recommend a novel from the latest autumn crop, and she answered, rather curtly, that it was hard to suggest a title just like that when you didn't know a reader's taste. I was about to reply but she cut me off.

"I recognize you, but we don't actually know each other, do we?"

I nodded, and I must have looked really let down, because she gave a little laugh and apologized for the rather abrupt way she'd spoken. In the end she pointed to one of those novels with a blatantly obvious plot, the kind that invariably has an upbeat ending. So I protested.

"No, uh-uh. Out of the question. I hate that sort of book."

She stepped back a few inches and let out another laugh, much more direct this time.

"I'm sorry. I'd forgotten that . . . Well, never mind. I have something else for you, Françoise."

I don't know if it was the fact she remembered my name, or that we were still the only people in the bookstore, but I suddenly felt free. Free in a way I hadn't in years. Free like when, as a child in my bedroom, I used to dream about what the future might have in store. It all came out, all of a sudden. How I admired her, for the path she had chosen. The way she managed her career, as an independent and intransigent woman. I told her she was a model for all the women who met her. Well, for me, in any case. She opened her eyes wide, gave a short, astonished laugh, began to stutter something then, frowning, asked me if this was a declaration of love. It didn't even throw me. I gave a sigh and said, "I would so have liked to be you."

The next time I dropped in, she told me we must say *tu* to each other. I had let a few days go by, immersing myself in the books she'd recommended. Standard, well-written stories, on the trail of famous artists. Michelangelo in Rome. Rodin in the midst of his creative fever. I went back to the bookstore with an aftertaste of something unfinished. What I wanted was the here and now, an encounter with characters of the sort I might meet in my everyday life. To get to the heart of their behavior. Share their anger, their frustrations, their hopes and joy. It wasn't escapism I wanted from my reading. I wanted to find my bearings again. I had lost them so long ago.

Lucie was silent for a few minutes, circling around the tables to pick up a book here and there. Without looking at me, she declared that the best thing would probably be for us to have lunch together someday soon. She would be better able to guide me—although, she added—she doubted I really needed any guidance. The back cover would suffice. My taste was much more confirmed than I realized. I immediately accepted her invitation, but we only got around to it two months later. We needed time to size each other up. She was increasingly cordial in the way she greeted me, but I could tell there was still a streak of defiance. I couldn't hold it against her. After all, no one sought out my company. I was one of those idle stay-at-home mothers who drifts through her life as if it were based on an American TV series from the 1950s. When I looked at myself in the bathroom mirror I didn't feel like trying to make friends with me, either. It was a crushing admission of failure—and no one at home had noticed. The only consolation, basically, was listening to the news and realizing how bad things were all over the planet. Twenty or thirty years from now everything would be finished. It would be a done deal.

We met up in the half-empty Mexican restaurant outside the center of town. It was the first time I'd ventured into that neighborhood. The proprietor greeted us warmly. Evidently Lucie was a regular. She ordered *fajitas* with *refritos* and I ordered the same, not really knowing what I'd be getting. It hardly mattered. I had the very clear sensation that I'd stepped outside my usual life, and I was both stunned and very honored. Above all, I was in Lucie's company—a situation I had so often fantasized about during my adolescence. I let my gaze wander over the exotic decor. I was on a little cloud. I crash-landed when Lucie declared that, actually, this lunch was a good idea, it would allow us to settle things once and for all. I looked her straight in the eye. She just stared back at me, not smiling.

"It's exactly as I thought. You have no idea what happened, do you?"

I didn't need to answer. It must have been enough to see the expression on my face. So there was a reason for this invitation—a serious reason. While I was trying to get my wits about me, dozens of images hurtled into one another before my eyes, including the faces of people I hadn't thought of in years, and, in a strangled voice, I muttered, "With what?"

Lucie sighed and nodded her head several times before answering with a question.

"With Léa and Guillaume?"

The relief. Instant. Selfish. Nothing to do with me. It was my son, and Lucie's daughter. An unhappy love story, no doubt. Guillaume didn't flaunt his success with women. He didn't need to. His father took care of that. He'd run into him several times on the arm of one of his conquests. He was inordinately proud; I had to force myself not to find this inappropriate. In the presence of guests Marc didn't hesitate to drop allusions that Guillaume pretended to deny forcefully, but I knew for a fact that they flattered his ego. These words I once heard in a film kept coming back to me: "When men are together, they're pathetic." That was it. Guillaume must have seduced Lucie's daughter then broken up with her in the brutal fashion I knew he was capable of. Lucie would have spent days on end consoling her daughter, and she had a grudge against Guillaume. Life, in other words. Across from me, she gave an ironic half-smile.

"And now you're imagining an affair gone wrong and a broken heart, because whether you like it or not, you're still a prisoner of your preconceived ideas."

Rape. That's what came to me just then. I immediately banished the thought. If there had been rape, Lucie would have urged her daughter to press charges. We would have heard about it. Or, it could be we were in that famous gray zone everyone was talking about at the moment. The moment when the woman hasn't given her consent and the man misunderstands. No. That's not the right way to put it. The moment when the man takes advantage of the woman's indecision. No. That's not it, either.

"It's nothing sexual, either, Françoise."

It was as if Lucie had been reading my thoughts. Was I really that transparent? I studied her. She took a deep breath then came out with it. She talked about bullying. The kind of harassment that attacks the soul, not the flesh. She told me about the daily humiliation, back when our children were in the same school. Guillaume was one of those star pupils whose name was on all the teachers' lips, whereas Léa tried to make herself as inconspicuous as possible. The insults. You're fat, ugly, dumb, you're a stupid bitch. Ostracized from parties.

Guillaume intimidated the other pupils so they wouldn't dare speak to the chosen prey. Phrases heard over and over, down every corridor: "Everyone hates you, don't you get it, everyone hates you." Shoulders hunched, hugging the walls, Léa searched for an explanation but couldn't find a single one. Before long she'd lost all self-confidence. Her grades plummeted. Her parents were worried. For weeks on end she wouldn't talk about it. And then all of a sudden she cracked. Lucie informed the administration, but the principal raised his eyebrows. He even went so far as to question Léa's statements, because, don't you know, Guillaume Leclerq, really, is a model student, he's always so eager to help. An excellent schoolmate. As for intellectually—let's not even go there, he's head and shoulders above everyone else.

Lucie said she could have made threats, taken the matter further, to the local media or the courts. But she didn't have the strength, and she was afraid her daughter would suffer even more. She'd end up dragging her story around like a millstone around her neck. They reached a compromise: a change of school, as discreetly as possible. In any case, it was out of the question for Léa to return to that middle school where her worst enemy ruled the roost. The rest of her time at school went smoothly enough, but her grades were never as brilliant as they had once been, before. Above all, it took her a long time to make new friends. She didn't trust anyone anymore.

"That was the worst, you see, Françoise. It wasn't so much about grades or popularity, I don't give a damn about all that and you know it. There are thousands of ways to flourish in life, and most of them don't have anything to do with obtaining some fancy diploma. But the loss of confidence, the subsequent fragility, that's hard to fight. Even with therapy. Even with the passage of time. She's fine now, thankfully, but I think if she were to see your son in the street, she'd go straight over to the other sidewalk rather than stand there in front of him and slap him in the face."

I stood up. Then sat back down. I tried to speak but nothing came out. I had a headache. I would have liked to stretch out on the tile floor and disappear. Or go a few hours back in time. A few weeks, even. To have never entered that bookstore. Which was ridiculous. Pretending not to know won't erase anything. What's important is to accept. And to make amends, when you can. That's what I was suggesting while the waiter was placing dishes I didn't remember ordering in front of me, and that I no longer felt like eating.

"I don't know what to say."

"Don't say anything, it's fine. To be honest, I was afraid you'd deny everything outright, and walk out slamming the door. I would have understood."

"I . . . I don't—I think this doesn't really come as a surprise to me."

"Did you suspect anything?"

"No, but . . . I can see the sort of man he's turning into. His bluntness. His loud laugh. The way he makes fun of people in their presence, insisting that it's all in good fun, of course. As if none of them would ever feel hurt. This sense he has that he's all-powerful. I . . . I have to meet Léa. I have to apologize to her."

"Françoise, Léa is grown-up now, like Guillaume, and she makes her own decisions. The only apology she would accept would have to come from Guillaume himself. And even then, I'm not sure. What she feels toward him now is fierce hatred. She won't forgive him. In fact, you know, part of the reason I didn't want to press charges was because I figured you didn't know anything about it. I remembered you from the lycée, and then I saw you from time to time in town, even though you didn't recognize me or were avoiding me, and you looked . . . How shall I put it . . . You looked kind."

"In a stupid sort of way?"

"No, that's the whole point. It's utterly ridiculous, assuming that if a person is kind they're bound to be stupid. There's not a drop of arrogance in you. I had the impression you felt empathy for others, and you didn't look on anyone with pity. And I was right."

"I didn't dare go up to you. Sometimes I would spend an inordinate amount of time trying to think of things to say, imagining meeting you. You've always really intimidated me. I would have liked to be as determined as you are. Less passive."

"We're all passive, Françoise. It's just we don't all follow the same path in life, or have the same arsenal."

My son is a scumbag. My son is a scumbag. My son is a scumbag.

"Madame, can I help in any way?"

The return to the present is brutal, and I don't immediately understand what this young man leaning over me—the waiter, or the owner, the one who's not called José, in any case—wants from me. I realize tears are flowing down my cheeks, spoiling my makeup. It's pathetic. I shudder. I wiggle on the banquette, while murmuring an apology. The young man says there's no reason to apologize. He's the one who has invaded my privacy, so he's the one who must apologize. I venture a timid smile, which must seem very wan. I say that his mother must be proud to have a son like him. He shrugs. He replies that he doesn't know, because they rarely see each other, and that's not the kind of conversation they have. But yes, that could be, in the end. He hopes above all that she's not too disappointed. She has been, in the past. Very disappointed. It's only recently that he—how to put it—changed his place in the world. Yes, that's it, he changed his place in the world.

"But why am I telling you my life story, anyway?" he adds, forcing a laugh. "I just wanted to make sure there was nothing you needed. I didn't mean to intrude."

"Do you mind if I sit here a little longer? I'll have another cup of tea. From the same teapot. It was very good."

He walks away. My cellphone rings. Guillaume. I let it go to voicemail. A few minutes later, my husband. I switch off the telephone. What Guillaume and his father will never understand is that it's my son I'm leaving, not so much my relationship with Marc. I don't want to hear anything about that boy ever again. About all his success. His exploits. I called Annabelle two days ago. I suggested we meet. She was wary, on the other end of the line. She told me clearly that it was out of the question for her to get back together with Guillaume, if that's what I was driving at.

"Not at all, Annabelle. I would just like to talk awhile with you. There are these gray zones I'd like to shed some light on."

A few seconds of silence—angels and demons passing. Then I continued the conversation.

"He's a monster, isn't he?"

And her reply, after a moment of hesitation.

"Yes. I think you could say that, yes."

On the banquette in the café I'm nodding my head to myself. I'm a crazy old woman following her train of thought, mumbling things. That young woman at the table in the back must be having a field day, if she likes drawing caricatures and exaggerating people's features.

CHLOÉ

I'VE STOPPED SKETCHING. From behind I can see the woman whose son suddenly rushed out a while ago. Her head is nodding like the little felt dog my father bought me at a gas station one day. You put it in the rear window of the car and that way, so my father explained to me, you can look at it and you won't get bored. It was a time when I was constantly begging for a kitten or a puppy, and my parents wouldn't hear of it, because it would "take a lot of looking after" and "it's always a song and dance to find someone to look after it when you go on vacation." I followed my father's advice that day and I watched the minidog nodding its head. I could feel the nausea welling up inside me. The sudden screech of tires. The vomit by the side of the road. My father, torn between annoyance, because this would lower his mileage average, and the satisfaction he got from refusing to take the highway, because, well, if this had happened on the highway, where you have to swerve in a panic onto the emergency shoulder, no sooner does the kid get out than a truck *whooshes* past at full speed and knocks her over and *wham*, she's dead.

I'm an only child. I regret it to this day. I could call my brother or sister and we'd plan to have lunch, where we could make fun of our parents. Well, of our mother, because she's the only one left. Make fun of her inconsistencies. Her fantasies of a new life.

A customer comes in and asks if she can sit out on the terrace now that the storm has passed. José grumbles that she can, but she'll have to wait awhile for him to set up the tables, and at the moment he's swamped; the woman hesitates for a few seconds then walks away without even saying goodbye. I glanced over at the other table that's occupied. Two men, roughly the same age. They've known each other for a long time, by the look of it. They're not really conversing. The first man is talking to himself and the other one is staring at him and smiling; in his eyes there's a strange mixture of tenderness and despair. I can hear snatches of what they're saying, because the one I can see only from behind doesn't hesitate to raise his voice. He must be used to speaking in public. He exudes self-confidence.

Ari was kind of like that. Very sure of himself. And at the same time more straightforward, colder. Finnish, in other words. That famous volcanic alliance of icy slopes and burning craters. If that gesticulating guy is the first to leave, later on, I just might go and say a few words to his companion. Congratulate him on his calm, impassive manner in the presence of so much verbal bluster. I'll confess that as far as his friend is concerned, the only thing you feel like doing is giving him a few good slaps in the face. Obviously, I won't. I'm not that sort of woman. I have no idea what sort of woman I am, either. Unattached. Someone who settled in the North, far away from here, and who came back neither richer nor poorer than before. I can still see Ari's face, his darting eyes, the little birthmark on his left cheek. Annika's hair, glinting red in the light. Their image stays with me for a few seconds then vanishes. Sometimes I manage to convince myself that they never existed.

I had a tearoom in Vantaa.

That's my magic formula, my mantra, when I'm feeling really down. Those six words bring back a host of images. My apron. The lemon meringue pie. The *mustikkapiiarkka*, a cross between a crumble and blueberry pie. The *pannukakku*—those pancakes that stick to your ribs. Mrs. Virtanen, who wanted me to call her Maija, and who couldn't understand why I still went on saying "Madam" to her, even though she was very old. Heikkinen, the upstairs neighbor, with his dog. Ari poking his head in the door and letting in the cold, freezing air. I would look up and see the passersby on their way to the shopping center. The buildings scattered around the square. Finnish cities are not very attractive. They aren't crumbling from the weight of monuments and relics, like French cities. They are grim. I felt good there all the same. My cocoon. Nothing bad could happen to me in the land of Father Christmas. I heard Annika's voice saying . . . No. Back to the present.

Oh, this time it looks like José has given up. He's sending his associate—well, his boss, if what I've heard is true. It's odd. It would be easier to picture José as the manager and Fabrice as the waiter. He doesn't use the same technique as his colleague. He wipes the tables around mine, which are already clean, then very casually he looks up and out the window at the street, and asks me quietly if I would like to order anything else, or if I'd rather be left alone. It's so unexpected that I'm thrown off-balance.

"Yes . . . Yes, of course. I hope I'm not too much of a bother. I . . . I get the feeling I really annoy your colleague."

"José? Oh don't worry about him. He moans a lot but he's a good guy. Well, he's my oldest friend, so I'm not objective."

"You handle the business together?"

He laughs. It's the word "handle" that amuses him, he says. As if we were talking about horses that needed taming. Or a sailboat threatened by a storm. Having said that, he adds, you're right, this last year it really was like a storm. We didn't know whether we'd be able to reopen. He apologizes for disturbing me with his twaddle, because I look very busy. I smile. I reply that I haven't heard the word twaddle in years—probably since grade school. It's the reference to school that gives me the courage to speak out.

"Your name is Fabrice Ortega, isn't it?"

He pauses. Stands there with the pink sponge in his hand, poised between worry and interest.

"Uh . . . Do we know one another?"

And then I picture the panic, the parade of faces and bodies in his mind, *Could it be that on one drunken night I might have slept with this girl, maybe we flirted at a student party, left the others, and I touched her breasts?* He blushes slightly and it makes him all the more likeable.

"No, not really. Well, yes, but we weren't, how do you say it, we weren't close or anything more than just acquainted. We were in the same Spanish class in middle school. Please, when I tell you my name, don't pretend you remember me, because I was a gray mouse who hugged the walls. You probably don't remember me at all."

"All right. But you still have to tell me who you are if you want me to have any sort of reaction."

"My name is Chloé. Chloé Fournier. You see, it doesn't remind you of anything. I wasn't very outgoing. That's still the case, actually, otherwise I wouldn't be sitting here in your back room."

"Well, you *are* sitting next to the picture window. You can see everything that's going on, inside and out."

I don't react to his words. Gradually, in Fabrice Ortega's features, I can see him as he used to be in class, when we were thirteen or so. He wasn't very talkative, either. But he enjoyed a certain popularity. Not too much, though. Let's just say that everybody seemed to appreciate him—which wasn't the case with me. I decide to push my luck, and realize that I'm having fun.

"You had this T-shirt you wore a lot and I was really envious. A view of Manhattan from the Brooklyn Bridge."

His face suddenly lights up. He remembers it perfectly. He'd actually had to fight for it, during the sales at the local superstore. Then he went around telling everyone it was his uncle who'd brought it back from the States. Back then you didn't say "États-Unis" or "USA," in French. You said "States" to the company at large—in English, just like that, in the middle of your sentence in French, and everyone else opened their eyes wide.

"And then one day you helped me with a math problem. Oh, just a few minutes in the corridor in building B, by the toilets."

He narrowed his eyes. That rang a bell, yes. A very hazy memory. The little tiles on the floor. Boys and girls constantly coming and going, mainly girls, who'd transformed the restrooms into a boudoir—their favorite subjects, boys, boys, and boys. Sometimes their periods, too. And yet, no matter how hard he tries, he can't call up that image of himself helping one of his classmates with a math problem. He panics. I reassure him.

"You see, I told you you wouldn't be able to remember me."

"I'm sorry."

"There's no reason to be. I've put a lot of effort into remaining inconspicuous. It was an exercise in noticeable identities."

He shifts from one leg to the other, his sponge in his hand. His mind is spinning at full speed, and yet nothing comes out.

"Normally, now, Fabrice Ortega, either you declare that you've been delighted to meet me but duty calls, and you rid yourself of the burden, or you ask me politely what I'm up to these days, and I will reply with a touch of mischief that I'm sitting in the café where you work, drinking one coffee after another so that you won't throw me out."

"No one's going to throw you out."

"Maybe you won't, but I'm not so sure about José."

"No, really, I promise. And anyway, I'm the one who decides."

"Sorry?"

"I'm the owner of this place."

He suddenly blushes bright red and mutters that he didn't mean to brag. He gets muddled in his excuses. I come to his rescue.

"The main thing is to know whether you like being the owner."

He shrugs. He replies that as for the property in itself, he's not so sure. On the other hand, he never thought he'd find it so fascinating to run a business. Including the aspects that seemed the most off-putting, like managing inventory and dealing with suppliers. He explains that originally, he thought he'd go into computers, it was an era where everyone was rushing to enroll in three-year bachelor's programs that offered words like "networks," "communication," and "virtual"—they thought companies would be hiring massively in those fields. Which wasn't entirely untrue, except that the jobs, in the end, were very repetitive and poorly paid. For a second he opens his eyes wide, seems to wake up suddenly, and apologizes again for bothering me with his chatter.

"Stop apologizing, Fabrice. I've always liked listening to other people. It relaxes me."

"That's also my favorite activity. So, as it happens, running a café is ideal."

At the last minute I bite my tongue to keep from saying that I can relate to that. I haven't spoken to anyone here about Vantaa. And I'm not about to begin with some vague acquaintance. At the same time, that's all I have left in this town—"vague acquaintances." I have no friends around here anymore. But it doesn't get me down. I like the idea that I'm just passing through.

"So, I didn't ask you what you're up to nowadays."

"And so, I couldn't answer that I sit doodling in cafés."

"You're an artist?"

"Sort of. Let's say I'm stuck in a sort of interlude I can't get out of."

"Because of the pandemic?"

"In part, yes. Before, I lived near Helsinki, in Finland."

I add the name of the country, because the few people I've talked to in the last eighteen months find it hard to locate the city on a map. The country, no. Scandinavia they can find, the Russian border. The vast expanses of forest and snow. They don't understand how someone could actually want to go and live in a place like that.

Fabrice Ortega lets out a short laugh and confesses that this is the first time he's ever met someone who has actually lived in Finland.

"Yes, I can imagine. Suddenly I take on this air of mystery. But in the end, it's like you running a café. At school you imagine your possible future but in the end you don't take the path you'd mapped out."

"May I offer you something? Tea? A . . . beer?"

"You can start by being less formal! But actually, I'm hungry, and I think I'll order a full breakfast with a Danish pastry, a double espresso, and orange juice, but please let me pay for it, otherwise your friend José will kill me on the spot. And besides, I have my dignity."

"I'll bring that right away. So I guess you—you'll be staying for a while, won't you?"

He turns on his heels, and I lose myself in contemplation of the drying surface of the road. The sky seems to be clearing and a few rays of sun are coming through. I resist the temptation to check my smartphone for the weather in Vantaa. I see Fabrice exchanging a few words with José, who is rolling his eyes. I must be the subject of their conversation. That hasn't happened to me in years. I should have ordered champagne.

JOSÉ

HE SLIPPED BEHIND the bar, gave a smile, and said, "She thinks you don't like her." I shrugged. I don't know the girl, so it's nothing to do with feelings.

"It's not her, it's her type."

"What type is that?"

"Someone who sits there for hours without ordering anything and pretends to be an artist, when she'd do better to get off her ass and find a job. That shouldn't be too hard. There are shortages everywhere—in the restaurant business, service industries, retail—and it'll get even worse if they stick us with a Covid passport or some bullshit like that."

Fabrice took a few steps back, frowning.

"You know, I think she's right. You really cannot stand her. Maybe you tried to hit on her at a nightclub and she sent you packing?"

"I was a bouncer, not a customer. I'm the one who would've thrown her out. And besides, no, she's really not my kind of woman. That sort of featherbrained 'I live on love and spring water and the money my parents give me every month,' really not my type."

"How in hell did you come up with such an idea?"

"She lives in the same neighborhood as my ex. Since the beginning of lockdown, in any case. A pretty nice house, even though it's starting to get old. A good plot of land. Apparently it all belongs to her mother, who moved somewhere with some guy who's much younger than her."

"Well listen to that, they've got Radio Gossip, the neighborhood where your ex lives!"

"You have no idea! If I remember correctly, she's back from some Nordic Podunk-upon-Fjord up there by the Arctic Circle. She gave no sign of life and then all of a sudden, wham, she shows up just when the government decides to close everything down. It's like all those shit-faced Parisians who leave their studios and scramble to shut themselves away at mom and dad's place, click goes the key, this is my house, it's all locked up, no one can come in."

Fabrice smiled and murmured that what he liked about me was my sense of humor and hyperbole. And the thing about him that always gets me is that he respects my opinion. And then his loyalty, of course. Loyal people are pretty thin on the ground. So, naturally, you lay down your weapons and surrender.

Besides, it's true: Everyone who went to study in Paris or elsewhere and claimed they were really making the most of that life they'd been dreaming of for years—all that culture there for the asking, the whirlwind of ideas and encounters, the spontaneous parties—all of a sudden they wake up one morning to this chilling piece of news: three days from now they'll be stuck in their tiny two-room apartment, in that shitty building which, yeah, maybe it does overlook the Canal Saint-Martin, but the plumbing is always blocked and the roof creaks. Those same people who used to come back here on the weekend and mouth off in every bar about how the provinces are hell on earth, everybody spying on everyone else, unbelievable how there's no entertainment besides the multiplex—well, they all came rushing back here, really happy after all that their parents still lived in this backwater they hated so much when they were growing up and which they openly made fun of the minute they went back to their El Dorado. They're the same people we'd see in the weeks after lockdown strolling along with their basket in hand on their way to the Arche Verte, the organic supermarket, then coming back out delighted because they'd discovered these fantastic pears that came straight from a local orchard. In the end they'd found something to like about their forced return. The problem, now and then, was having to live with their parents who, frankly, didn't dwell in the same time zone. And then there was the Internet connection, too. It's unbelievable they don't have fiber optic everywhere in this country nowadays.

To them that whole lockdown time was some sort of vacation. But not for us. I had just broken up with my ex. I had to move, but everything started happening so fast, and I hardly had time to think. I panicked. There was no way I could go back to the neighborhood where I was born, even though I'm proud of it. To be shut away inside a six-story apartment block where the noise never stops and the walls are made of papier-mâché, with parents who are clueless about how to act around a son they thought they'd gotten rid of—no way. It was Fabrice who bailed me out, yet again. He lives on the other end of town, in a big apartment in a quiet building that looks out onto a park, with fields in the distance, and it's half-empty because, in the end, it doesn't suit most people: too far from the center and the shopping areas, too expensive for the neighborhood, not practical enough, no balcony—people would rather fork out a little more and buy a house in the suburbs outright, at least you're in your own home. Two days after the president's announcement, Fabrice told me that if I didn't have anywhere to go by the following week, I could move in with him. There were two bedrooms, and a big living room; it was a bit far from everything, but you can't always have it all. We could go jogging in the park across the street. I didn't even know what to say. I wished I could take him in my arms. Embrace him. Cry, even. All I managed to say was some jibe about guardian angels. I added, with a sort of grunt so that he'd understand I was being ironic, that he was saving my bacon. I wasn't being ironic, though. Anything but. For the second time, Fabrice was coming to the rescue. The following evening I arrived with two bags, a suitcase, and my guitar. We went shopping in a packed supermarket, with no social distancing whatsoever. When we got home we collapsed on the sofa. We were ready.

I'd been flattered that, before lockdown, he'd thought of me to help him out when he took over Le Tom's. I remember when I got the message. It was a Sunday. I kept telling myself I would have to leave the bar where I was working—and that sooner or later I'd have to tell Tiphaine about my family. About my past. I couldn't go on lying to her. I was feeling blue, and that sapped my energy. All of a sudden Fabrice's words came on the screen, and the day lit up. I replied right away that he could count on me. I wondered, all the same, how he'd managed to find the money to buy the business. I swore I'd ask him about it some day, but then in the end I never had the guts. I suppose he has a banker in his family or that his folks are well-connected. That's what's divided us since childhood, Fabrice and me: We weren't born on the same side of the bypass. On one side, the projects—apartment blocks that need regular repainting to hide the graffiti and that are occasionally torn down when they get insalubrious; the stadium surrounded by a park that fills with people mainly around sunset, the swimming pool where the "wi" was missing from the sign, so that we all laughed whenever we had to say, "we can't, we're on our way to the *smming* pool." On the other side of the bypass was one of those suburban zones built in the 1960s and which must have tripled in surface these last twenty years, eating away at the fields and the old farms that used to be there. A labyrinth of traffic circles and one-way streets where driving school instructors love to bring their beginners to get them lost. Fabrice's parents invested in their house early on, they enlarged it, bought a neighboring plot—in short, they had nothing to complain about. Their garage was even big enough to hold parties on

Saturday evenings. I was never invited to any of those parties. Fabrice and I weren't childhood friends. We just went to
the same schools because Fabrice's parents wanted nothing to
do with the priests, even though all the neighbors' kids took
the bus to the private school. We watched each other grow
up. We also belonged to the same basketball team in school,
and he was better at it than I thought he'd be. He knew
how to weave in and out and make critical passes. When it
came to free throws, that was another matter. And so, that
should have been the end of the story. But there was Yasmine.
Yasmine made it clear to us, individually, that she was hesitating. Between the two of us. That she was losing sleep over it.
What a coincidence, so were we. We were sixteen.

And then came more trouble, in the form of an episode
one Friday evening as we were leaving the lycée. On the far
side of the bypass bridge. They were blocking the sidewalk on
the Rue de Lattre de Tassigny—the entrance to my neighborhood. There were three of them. They were a few years older
than I was. I knew them well. I let out a groan. I'd figured
that sooner or later they'd notice I'd been taking a commis-
sion on the bars of hash. The ones I was supposed to be selling for them. Lately I'd been a little greedy with the margins.
I wanted to buy some clothes that would really stand out. I
wanted to wow Yasmine. Make her lean toward my side of
the scale, and not to the side of the guys who had all the luck
right from the start because they lived in a proper house with
a garage where they could throw parties—even though I'd
heard, how pathetic, that Fabrice's mother would come and

look in from time to time to make sure they weren't drinking too much alcohol and that the music wasn't too loud.

Normally, this is how events should have unfolded: They would smash my face in. Once I was a real mess, with my clothes torn and my nose all bloodied, I would swear on my mother's life that I would reimburse the money I owed, with interest, of course. They'd probably give me a deadline of two weeks, roughly—and then I'd have to come up with something creative, otherwise, for a few weeks, or months, or even years, I'd be a slave to L., the neighborhood boss. The three of them were waiting for me, unruffled, with that little smile that is the worst sort of threat. I thought about my ribs. My swollen face. The impossibility of seeing Yasmine for a while. The lies I'd have to come up with, which she wouldn't believe. And as a result, she'd go straight to the other guy. Calmer. Above all, more reassuring, even though it was annoying, the way he never finished his sentences. She's the one who told me that. As if his thoughts never went further than three suspension points. I'd laughed. I had this determined side she liked. I knew where I was headed. I took a deep breath and crossed the bridge. It would have been pointless to take to my heels and try to hide—I had nowhere to go, for a start, and besides, they'd find me sooner or later, and then they'd be even more on edge.

T., the one who'd given himself the role of Mr. Nice Guy, explained the situation. It was like something out of those TV programs my mother was crazy about: a courtroom, a defendant, a lawyer. Except that there was no lawyer and the verdict was going to be hasty. I owed them six hundred euros, plus three hundred in interest, nine hundred. Did I have it on me? No? So what are we gonna do?

I didn't have time to answer. Out of nowhere, Fabrice appeared beside me, with his physique like a wet cat. I stood there gaping. The others, too. Where had he come from, this rookie who couldn't mind his own business? He started speaking. You almost expected him to pull out a notebook and begin writing down what was said. He wanted to know what the problem was, and that cracked them up, the other three. T. even started laughing when he asked, Who is this clown? Never taking my eyes off the three of them I advised Fabrice to continue on his way. He didn't move.

"How much do you owe them?"

"Nine hundred."

The words came out all on their own. It was only afterward that I realized that in fact, he'd known exactly what was going on. He probably knew about the drug dealing. He'd been keeping an eye on me. This time, the other three laughed all at once. Who is this guy? Is he your lover? Are you a fag? Does he wear the pants? Do you get paid to sleep around, too?

Fabrice didn't get flustered. He began negotiating. Asking when the sum had to be paid to avoid a bloodbath. He used these ridiculous expressions that sounded like something out of a bad TV movie, and the other three kept on snickering, but they answered all the same. I wished he would go away and leave me alone with the shit I'd created for myself, but I couldn't get a word in edgewise. I became a witness to some sort of mind-boggling verbal jousting. In the end they agreed on Friday, same time, different place, more discreet, the entrance to the parking lot, no one would notice an envelope changing hands. One of the members of the trio complained—it would still be a lot easier to meet somewhere in the projects, but Fabrice held his ground: It was better for everyone concerned to exchange the merchandise in neutral territory. I couldn't see how it was better for anyone, but he had so much calm self-assurance, something I'd never noticed, that the others caved. They went off, even forgetting to shower us in insults. Once they'd turned the corner I said, "What the hell was that all about?"

"You're in deep shit. I came to help."

"I didn't ask you for any favors."

"I hate unfair fights. I saw you from across the street. Three against one, that's a massacre."

"You're hoping I'll leave you a clear field with Yasmine in exchange, is that it?"

"Yasmine will choose whoever she wants, and for all we know, it might be neither one of us. Well, let's not stand here forever!"

"Okay, you're the king of making plans, aren't you? So what next?"

"We go for a piss and then to the bank."

"What?"

"That gave me the willies, José. And not just a little. When I get the willies I always need to go for a piss."

"You said the bank?"

"I have a savings account. The kind where you put the money your grandparents and your uncles and aunts give you at Christmas and for your birthday, and your parents deposit a small amount every month so you can get your driver's license and make the monthly payments on your first car."

"Thanks, I know what a savings account is. Even if I don't know anyone who has one. And you're going to ask for nine hundred euros, and they're going to hand it to you, in cash, you're going to give it to me and that's it?"

"Precisely. In two installments, since I'm not allowed to take out more than a certain amount each day."

"What do you expect in return?"

"Listen, I'm about to burst. We'll talk about all that when my bladder's empty. I'm going for a piss."

We didn't really bring up the subject again. We kind of skirted the issue. That's when I came to know one of Fabrice's great strengths: He may stay in the background, but he still notices everything, he listens, he observes, and then all of a sudden he goes into action. He's not at all the dilettante you might take him for. He's incredibly efficient for a few days, and then he withdraws again, but by then life has changed radically. In any case, my life changed radically. At the teller's window in the bank he was smiling and sure of himself. When the employee asked him, ever so casually, whether he had a sizeable purchase to make, he calmly replied that he didn't think he was obliged to answer that type of question, and the other guy went bright red. The nine hundred euros

were still a loan, but with no interest. I would pay him back
bit by bit, when I had a job over summer break or even later.
There was no rush. Otherwise, there were no demands on
me. He didn't lecture me. He didn't tell me to stop dealing
or hanging out with that sort of people. He said, more than
once, that he wasn't my big brother, or any other member of
my family. He was getting me out of a tough spot because he
could, and because, if Yasmine was hesitating between the
two of us, it was probably because we had more in common
than we realized. I'd never looked at it that way. It was more
like I'd been in a boxing ring with an adversary I had to beat.
That week I realized you could always find another way to
deal with a problem. I haven't forgotten it.

The worst thing was that he turned out to be right, across
the board. In the end, Yasmine refused to choose between us,
and a few weeks later she moved away to be with her sister
in Lyon. She disappeared off the radar and I would have felt
it was a huge loss if it hadn't been for the sight of Fabrice,
how I'd run into him fairly regularly. We would wave. Smile
at each other. One day he saw me with a basketball in my
hands. I suggested he come along—we'd been members of
the same team a few years earlier, after all.

I went to practice my shots on the court next to the lycée.
We stayed there nearly two hours, as day faded into evening.
In the beginning we didn't talk about anything special. Then
gradually I gave him advice about his free throws, which were
still his weak point. The conversation went on to memories
of middle school, our respective neighborhoods, what we

planned to do next. We found out that both of us were thinking of enrolling in short-term business courses, accountancy
for him, and marketing for me. Neither of us really knew
why, and it made us laugh. I started to bring up my debt
but he shook his head and said, "When the time comes, if it
comes." Since then we've never really lost touch. We've kept
an eye on each other.

That summer, after the baccalaureate, I found a deadly
boring but fairly well-paid job, bagging the shopping for customers at the superstore who'd preordered online; I put their
bags first on a pallet, then in the trunk of their car when they
came to collect it. I met different people. I learned how to
go about finding a reasonably cheap studio, and how to make
the most of the social welfare benefits. My parents never filled
out the forms. They were perpetually convinced that no matter
what, they had no right to anything. I paid back half the sum
I owed Fabrice, and he set aside a small amount from it to take
me out for a pizza. I didn't tell him it was the first time I'd ever
been to a real restaurant. I got the impression that doors were
now opening up to me, doors I never even knew existed.

What I don't really get is what happened to us next—
separately. We finished studying for our respective diplomas,
and obtained one short-term contract after another that
never turned into anything permanent. We even agreed to do
internships. We would stand around for hours waiting our
turn at the employment office. We were *searching actively*, the
way the exhausted agents sitting across from us had told us to
do; they didn't believe any more than we did in our chances

of success. I gave up before he did. I needed to move out of my parents' place, out of the neighborhood I'd grown up in. I took the sort of jobs that deprive you of any sort of social life—nightclub bouncer, security guard at an underground parking lot—so when I was offered a position as a waiter in a café, I jumped at the chance, even though everyone knew that the boss was a piece of shit who was constantly trying to eat away at your pay while he spent his time watching your every move so that he'd have plenty of pretexts to find fault and yell at you once your shift was over. It didn't matter. The pay wasn't too bad, for once. I could hang on to the one-bedroom place I'd found in the center of town, where the rent was really reasonable, because nobody wanted to sleep in an apartment that was just above a pedestrian street. The minute it started to get warm, with the windows open and all the sidewalk cafés and restaurants, it was hell. You couldn't get to sleep before four or five in the morning, which was just when the garbage truck came thundering down the street. I didn't stay there long. I met Tiphaine. It wasn't complicated. She worked at the clothes store a little farther up the street— some major international brand that drew a crowd during the sales. She rose quickly through the ranks, and now she was running the place. We would meet every morning at the Potron-Minet, a café located away from all the commotion. We had the same habit: have our breakfast while reading the local and regional papers. Like an old couple. We would swap papers with a smile. One day I asked her what sign of the zodiac she was. I read her horoscope out loud. She was about to meet a man she must keep at a distance, because he would probably ruin her life the way he was already ruining her rare morning moments of peace and quiet. For a few seconds she believed it and opened her eyes wide, exclaiming, "Really?" I knew at once that we'd be together for a while.

Two years.

Two years is both long and short. Time enough to get into habits. To get to know every fold and wrinkle on the other person's skin. Their smell. Their tics. The way they spent their days off in a T-shirt, size XXL, sitting on a stool by the window watching the world go by, drinking gallons of coffee. She lived in a magnificent apartment with a view onto the square facing the cathedral. I moved in after six months. I didn't have many friends; she did. I slipped gently into her world. It was the most comfortable place I'd ever lived. My only regret was that Tiphaine's dreams went no further than vacation in Greece or Ibiza. Partying. Heat. Crowds. I dreamed of roaming through vast expanses of wilderness, and meeting people—in Scotland, the Andes, or the depths of Asia. She made fun of me the first time we went on vacation together, because it was my maiden flight. She couldn't believe there were people who had never been on an airplane. When I talked to her about my family, I made things up. Which was disgraceful, sure. I told her I'd grown up on the right side of the bypass. In a suburban house. Near Fabrice's place. She wanted to meet my parents—but they lived far away. They'd gone back to Portugal, where they were from. They had a white house in the Algarve. She wanted to go there. I shrugged. Later.

I got tangled up in my lies. I convinced myself that I was waiting for the right moment to tell her the truth, but deep down I was realistic and knew that I had my fucking head in the sand. I was waiting for the disaster. It would strike in the shape of my mother; we ran into her in one of those shopping districts where normally she never went, under any circumstance. She inspected Tiphaine from head to toe and asked me straight out when I meant to come and visit them, it had been that long. While she was chatting away, I kept thinking that it was nothing, I'd be able to make her out to be a slightly unpleasant aunt that I didn't want to see. Then out she came with, "It's your father's birthday soon, I hope you'll be there this time." She walked away, in her dress with its pattern of big pink and blue flowers and her worn-down shoes. The image of her still wakes me up at night. I'm back there, in that no man's land of consumerism, store after store, sale after sale, bumper-to-bumper customers everywhere, thirsting for a bargain, running from one special offer to the next. The sudden nausea that came over me. My silence when, after a few steps, Tiphaine stopped and asked me if I was going to explain it to her. I didn't know where to begin. The only thing I felt like doing was walking straight ahead, getting out of that procession of boutiques, crossing the main road and continuing on, into the fields, and disappearing.

Of course the truth came out eventually, but it was final—and I couldn't hold it against Tiphaine. I understood all her arguments—how could she trust me now, when I'd been hiding my background, what was I thinking, that she couldn't fall in love with a kid from the projects, did I have such a low an opinion of her, yes, and while we're at it, actually, what did I really think of her? Was she a pretentious little bougie who held her nose whenever she walked past people whose background was foreign?

I almost laughed. Because of the expression "foreign background." All the people I'd grown up with were born here. Their parents, too. There was no more background. People sometimes yelled at them to go back to their village, but everyone knew that was just idle talk. Even vacations back in the old country were becoming rare. Except for the Kosovars or the Croats, who'd come here more recently. Your background was the neighborhood you'd grown up in.

She was waiting for an answer. I didn't have one. The television was on the nonstop news channel. The presenters were wearing a glum expression, as usual. This new virus that had come from some Chinese animal no one had ever heard of, and which had escaped from a market in Wuhan, was forcing entire regions to shut themselves up at home. In Italy they had cases. The president and the prime minister with his salt-and-pepper beard were about to make an official statement. The word "lockdown" was on everyone's lips. It was only a matter of days. Tiphaine glanced at the news and gave a sigh. She added that she was sorry, but she couldn't possibly stay locked up with someone who had deceived and disappointed her to such an extent. I could just go home to my parents. Apparently, they were eager to see me.

A few weeks before that I'd had a message from Fabrice.

He was looking for someone to be his "first mate"—I remember how I smiled, because no one but him uses expressions like "first mate." He had just put in a bid on a café—if ever I was interested. I called him back right away. I couldn't stand working for that piece-of-shit boss anymore. We visited the premises together. The café was clean, but it had seen better days. It belonged to an old woman who'd taken Fabrice under her wing, so it seemed. She was looking for a successor, someone she could trust. There were no major drawbacks to worry about. Fabrice and I pictured the changes we could make so that the café would look like our place. We made plans. I quit my job. It was December 2019. We figured we could take over the business without touching a thing for the moment, and that we'd renovate during summer vacation. Both of us knew craftsmen who could give us a hand, at an unbeatable price. Three months later my love life had gone belly-up, and I was out on the street. All nonessential businesses were going to have to close, they said, and the State would provide funding to help maintain employment. I felt like an animal in a cage. And then Fabrice with his unflappable composure came along, suggesting I spend lockdown with him—the apartment was plenty big for two.

"What exactly is your role in my life? Are you my guardian angel?"

That was my reply. He smiled. He gave a shrug. He went on as if nothing had changed.

There we were a few days later, the two of us, on his sofa until the middle of the night watching one TV series after another, mixing up the plots. Fabrice got up early to go running in the park across the street and I eventually did the same. A cute little couple. That's what the cashiers at the superstores must have thought, when we went there together to do our shopping. In the beginning I felt like telling everyone that we weren't a couple, but after a while I let it go. Nobody cared, and besides, it didn't bother me if people thought I was sharing my life with him—because I was.

Since the café was closed, we decided to start on the renovations. We sanded and scraped, repainted, redid the floors. We changed the stools. The only thing we couldn't change were the black leatherette banquettes. We'd run out of funds and energy. They're still clean, but pretty worn, and you can see they've had their day. We tried to convince ourselves they looked vintage. The more I look at them, the more I tell myself we were wrong.

When we reopened last summer, with QR codes in place of menus, and the requirement to wear masks indoors, we were afraid customers wouldn't come back. Some did change their watering hole, but others came in their place. A younger clientele, noisier, too—the neighbors called the police a few times and we had to spell things out to get a few of the rowdier patrons to calm down, in particular some friends of that guy who was here awhile ago with his mother and who walked out on her, leaving her to her tea and her whims about teapots. The main thing is that we got through it. And then everything went crazy again. It wasn't even the end of autumn when they imposed the curfew. That really got us down. I was still living with Fabrice, but the atmosphere was oppressive—we'd go back to his apartment in the evening feeling frazzled from the day's tension. When I heard a friend was moving I seized the opportunity to take over his lease and regain my independence. When I broke the news to Fabrice, he reproached me for not letting him know. I answered that I'd been hinting at leaving for several weeks already, but he didn't seem to have heard me. I thought the discussion was going to turn sour, but we looked at each other, and buried the hatchet. We knew the situation had always been temporary, and besides, it wasn't as if we didn't see each other during the day. At one point, Fabrice put his hand on my shoulder and came out and said he'd had a very good lockdown in my company. I replied that it was time for him to find someone else. To put himself back on the market. Nearly thirty years old. Restaurant owner. Spacious apartment. They'll be lining up in droves.

It hasn't happened, though. That's the whole tragedy of people who work in the restaurant business—they see tons of people, but those people hardly notice them, and then their working hours really mess with their social life. When you get off work at three o'clock in the morning, your eardrums throbbing from the shouting and the music, all you want is to go to sleep. The last thing you want is to talk. That's why I want to get out of this business, too. Like so many others, after these strange months we've been through. Not just workwise, either. Everything else, too. The town. The country. The continent. Years have gone by without me even realizing, and I've never been out of this region, except for a week or two on overcrowded Mediterranean beaches. I'm done with that, now. Thanks to cohabitation with Fabrice, I've saved enough to go away for two or three months—and then, as a waiter, who's French, who can cook, I know I can get a job anywhere. When I was little, I put a map of the world above my desk and often I would say, over and over, the names of the places I wanted to visit when I was grown up. Dundee, Loja, Copenhagen, Cape Town, Osaka, La Paz. It's time for me to fulfill my dream. What am I waiting for? Honestly? For a start, for all this coronavirus crap to be over with so we can move around as we see fit without being afraid of yet another last-minute lockdown. And then, until I'm sure someone will take over here, after me. So that Le Tom's will keep going. So Fabrice won't suffer from my desertion. So that Fabrice won't suffer, period.

That's why I don't trust that pseudoartist over there. With her faux goody-goody air and her unexplained return from the Far North. I don't trust her. At last we have a little freedom again and she goes and shuts herself away at the back of a café? Honestly, what is her problem?

Oh, the local writer—I can't stand him, either, you only have to see the way he blows his own trumpet in the newspaper, it's unbearable—he wants another coffee. A double. The guy who's with him shakes his head, smiles at me, no nothing for him, thanks. A glass of water, maybe. If it's no bother. For a moment I feel caught in his gaze—an ocean of gentle sadness.

PIERRE VILLIERS, 57—TABLE NO. 2

(first row on the right, next to the picture window)

I'M SMILING. I can't stop smiling. I wonder if tomorrow morning my jaw will ache. I'm smiling because I'm happy to see him. I'm smiling, too, because he's delivering a monologue that totally excludes me. He's like a lumberjack, hewing sentences like little logs. I'm impressed. I don't know if he realizes he's the only one making a sound in this peculiarly quiet café, and that he's probably disturbing the others. The young woman at the back who's drawing. The two waiters, or the waiter and the proprietor, impossible to tell who's in charge of whom. The woman on the other side of the row of tables, who dismissed her son so abruptly awhile ago. I heard everything, while Thibault continued to spout his litany. I had to admire her. I still admire her. There she sits, alone with her cup of tea and the huge teapot she asked for, gently but firmly. I think I would have liked to have had a mother like her.

I'm smiling, but I'm not even sure he's noticed. He's going on and on about the different adaptations of his works, and the auctions that were held among several publishers to acquire his latest novel. I read it, the way I've read all his books since I saw in the local paper that he'd fulfilled his dream of becoming a writer. It's always hard to give your opinion of someone's work when you know them personally. Everything gets skewed. You look for yourself in each of the characters. You make suppositions. You wonder if this family name isn't hiding another. You end up getting disoriented and losing the plot. Often when I start reading one of his books I have to stop at around page fifty and start everything over from the beginning because I've lost the thread. But anyway. I thought the last one was labored. That's the word that immediately sprang to mind. You can sum up the plot in two sentences and it takes him over three hundred pages to churn it out. Naturally, I'm no expert and it's probably the style that holds it all together, but, I don't know, it's the first time I've been a little disappointed. Now I can see why, given that the stream of words hasn't dried up. He's become verbose. Maybe he always has been, deep down.

I remember the day I saw his portrait splashed across the front page of the regional daily, five or six years ago. There he was, with that ironical half smile. He was also splashed across pages two and three, in a marathon interview. The prodigal son, returning to the fold. To his "territory," as they like to call it nowadays. Before, it was referred to as the provinces. Or even the place where the hicks lived. But "territory" is so much better. Like the former overseas territories, but in the home country. People come here on "city breaks" for a weekend, and they admire the timbered houses, the seven churches, the cute little pedestrian streets. Still, they're happy to leave again on Sunday afternoon, because honestly, to live in this sort of big market town, you'd have to do without so many pleasures, even if there is Wi-Fi everywhere.

I read the article. Two, three, four times over. The sentences dug trenches in my brain. Tears rose to my eyes and I rushed out of my office to hide in the restroom. I stared at my reflection in the mirror above the sink for a long time. I couldn't calm the whirlwind of emotions that had taken hold of me. Everything was thoroughly mixed up.

There was jealousy, of course—because all of us somehow dream of the limelight. I suppose I wasn't the only one. Everyone who's ever crossed paths with Thibault must be drooling with envy. But admiration, too, for the courage that I didn't have, the courage to leave everything behind and start a new life. There was nostalgia, obviously, for those years when I was the sun the other planets revolved around. I went to the lycée to shine. I basked in the other students' admiration. I was tall and slim with dark hair and very black eyes, and the perfect earring—I was edgy, too, enthusiastic, cheerful. Irresistible. I loved the way my classmates looked at me. Thibault in particular. An adoration that troubled and excited me at the same time. To the point of making me wonder which way my preferences lay. I tried playing with fire. I didn't always succeed. I can look at it clearly now. I know how brutally I must have behaved. The worst thing was that I was aware of the suffering I caused him.

I thought hard all day after reading the article, and then I threw myself into the trap. A moth fluttering around a burning bulb. I wanted his company. Through social media I sent him dozens of messages. It was pathetic. I hated myself for reacting that way, but I couldn't change my attitude. It took him some time to reply to my friend request on Facebook, and once he accepted—probably with a sigh of hopelessness—he threw me only a few crumbs of his attention. A few onomatopoeias. One sentence. Later, through force of habit, I even got a few meetings out of him. Always very brief. A coffee, on the run. A beer in the back room between six and seven. He was toying with my weakness. He was right. It was a brilliant revenge. It was my wife who set me straight again. One evening she asked me what I hoped to achieve, exactly. I shrugged. I didn't really know, in the end.

It's not important. It was long ago, all that. I don't know if he has realized how much distance I've put between us. The message he sent me is clear: you're nothing in my life, you're insignificant. Deep down I'm grateful to him for that. I've been thinking a lot, since then. Above all, during these last two years. I've had the time, all those nights when I lay awake because of the corticosteroids. Those days when I was just waiting for my downfall, my end.

I hesitated a long time before posting that photograph of the two of us, two days ago. I knew he'd see it—he's on social media a lot more than he lets on in his interviews. I could imagine how annoyed he'd be, on the other side of the screen. And then, I figured I had no reason to censor myself. After all, that period had existed, whether he liked it or not. Besides, I wasn't really thinking about him when I put us on display, insolent and united in the brilliance of youth. I was thinking about Sophie. The girl who had taken the photo. I remember it was a few days before the party she had at her place. She gave me the print once Thibault had already left for Paris and we no longer had any news of him. We talked about him. How attractive he was. About my attitude. She was very frank with me. She forced me to see something I didn't want to look at. My ambivalence. My dithering. My malice, too. I'd enjoyed the conflict between us. We became an item for a few months after that, but she was too rational and too honest. I needed to shine in my partner's eyes in those days, and with her the dazzle was too dull. We parted on good terms. She invited me to her wedding, a few years later. I was really surprised. We were barely twenty-five years old. None of our friends were getting married. I declined the invitation. I shouldn't have, but there are so many things that we shouldn't do. I tried to find her when Thibault came back into my life. I needed that sharp gaze of hers. I couldn't find her. It's strange how people can still disappear so easily, even though we leave virtual traces practically everywhere we go. I couldn't remember her married name. I gave up for a while, promising myself I'd have another go—and then life overwhelmed me. And death, above all.

I must have been making a strange face, because he abruptly interrupted his soliloquy.

"Are you all right?"

"Yes, sorry. I switched off. I—"

"Tired?"

"Yes, that's it. I had a bad night."

"Same here."

I smile. Nearly dislocating my jaw. It isn't really the same, Thibault, no. For a few seconds, all we hear is the sound of the coffee machine and, faintly, in the background, the radio playing a song I instantly recognize. The Verve. "Bitter Sweet Symphony." Indeed. Between the two of us there is more that's bitter than sweet, but that doesn't matter anymore. I'm not your opponent, Thibault. I think you still haven't worked that out. Nor am I your vassal. I'm sitting here across from you. Your eyes dart around and never pause on my face. Look at me. Stare at me for a long time. You'll see. You won't regret it.

This is probably the last time we'll get together, Thibault, but you clearly haven't sensed that. We should get closer, sweep aside the rules of social distancing that have been poisoning us for months. I would put my head on your shoulder and gaze out at the street. A few people in the café might raise their eyebrows, but no one would be really offended. That's all in the past, now.

In the past. I know it. I held the gaze of my hematologist, Laurent, while he was talking, and suddenly he began to stammer. That was when I understood. Maybe even before. Because it had come back. Do you remember Laurent? He was in our class at the lycée. We used to make fun of him because he spent all his time slogging away at math and physics instead of enjoying the summertime of life. After my wife and my daughters, he's probably the person I'm closest to now.

I clench my jaw briefly, but you don't notice. It's just that when there's any mention of my children, I can't stop the tears. But I've learned to control them and to keep on smiling—even though sometimes a grimace isn't far away. The girls don't know yet. Anna doesn't want to tell them. She keeps delaying the inevitable, but she won't be able to hold out much longer. Louise, our eldest, is in her final year of med school. When she comes to visit, she asks very precise questions, and she examines me, under the guise of cuddles. She hasn't been back since March but she plans on coming next week. I won't be able to fool her for very much longer, given her professional eye. The only people I can still fool are the ones who don't really look at me: passersby in the street, waiters in cafés, checkout attendants at the supermarket, the teller at the bank—and you, Thibault.

I had only a few months' remission. Relapse is frequent, with blood cancer. Laurent assured me that the second barrage of treatments was bound to work, but I don't believe in it anymore. The first time, I began my treatment like a conqueror, and even though I subsequently lost my illusions—because no matter how you imagine it, you're still at the mercy of the side effects of the chemo—I went through the ordeal with my head held high. That was the expression that was lodged in my mind. *Head held high*, with the notion that the illness would not beat me. It's kind of ridiculous, don't you think? Very presumptuous, in any case.

Now, when I think about the treatment and all the time I'm still going to have to spend alone in my hospital room, all those nights wondering why me, why now, why so young, I just feel tired. My daughters are grown up, they're both in relationships with gentle, understanding young men, they'll manage. It will be a bit harder for Anna, of course. All the time we shared, suddenly reduced to vacation snaps, and the songs we used to listen to together—she always had a soft spot for Delpech and for the Stone Roses. I hope she'll be able to cope. That Laurent will help her through the ordeal. Laurent often knows what to say, to console and encourage. The last time we met, he was more hesitant. He didn't finish his sentences. No need to spell it out. From tomorrow on I won't be leaving the house except to go to the hospital. You're my last outing, Thibault.

I'm making the most of this stolen interlude, while you know nothing about its singular importance. You're still holding forth. You've always loved that. In your dreams I was the hero of your adolescence, a heavenly tramp, flamboyant and boastful, but you were kidding yourself. I was nothing like the portrait you wanted to paint of me, but naturally I went along with it, because it made me look better in my own eyes. I bathed in the light you cast over me. Yes, I was more clear-eyed than you thought. I could tell that the laurels of words you wove for me would soon wither, and that you would continue on your way, even if it was treacherous. It would give you greater clarity, but not necessarily a smile. The smile is mine. However much I may have forced it when I first came into the café, it now seems to me to have reverted to its natural state. I have creases at either side of my lips because I have loved this life in spite of everything. And crow's-feet at my eyes, because I've spent too much time squinting, taking such a narrow view of the universe, while you were off exploring other worlds.

What do you know! That's precisely what you're talking about now. The trips you've taken. The translations of your books, which have brought you invitations from all over the world. You're spluttering, and I'm not afraid of the droplets from your saliva. Nothing can touch me now. I sit across from you and listen. It will be a fine memory, Thibault. You'll often think back on this moment. You'll start your sentences with these words: "I had no idea it was the last time we'd meet." With a bit of bad luck, you might even write a whole novel about it.

12:00 P.M.

JOCELYNE

WHEN I WALKED IN, Fabrice wanted to come up and say hello, but I gave a wave to dissuade him. I didn't want to start talking before I'd had time to get my bearings. The three steps leading up to the back room look nice. Fabrice had warned me that they had redesigned the entire layout. The room I had used for storage and supplies has disappeared. The walls have come down. A picture window now floods the café with light. It's nice. I'm not surprised, because I got the photos he sent during lockdown, but it's always better to see things with your own eyes. A pity they didn't change the leatherette banquettes. Still, apart from that, there are no errors of taste. They were right to replace the beige tiles with hardwood floors—with a trap door leading to the cellar, it gives you the impression the place has always been here, a brilliant idea. Customers will be convinced they're in a centuries-old wine bar, yet I recall that when I was little this place was a fishmonger's. You can make people believe anything.

I didn't tell Fabrice I'd be coming. I wanted to catch him in his element—and see how he behaves. There still aren't a lot of people, but you can tell the terrace will be full by lunchtime, now that the storm has passed. They'll be pulling around the chairs and the tables, calling to one another, talking about their recent or imminent vacations. They might be sixteen, thirty-two, fifty-four, or seventy-three years old, they'll drink red ale, mint cordial and soda, or Coke (and there will surely be some girl who'll claim she can tell Coke from Pepsi, blindfolded if need be). People will burst out laughing, tell a few risqué jokes, make a few caustic comments, then shout for joy on seeing another group of friends headed their way. The terrace is a slice of life.

That's where she ought to be sitting, that young woman. Well no, of course not, not with all her stuff—sketchbook, pens, felt tips. What I like about being the age I am now, and about my situation, is that I no longer have to worry about convention—if I ever did; it's not my style.

"May I sit here?"

She widens her eyes slightly, but nods. Her face is very childlike when it comes alive. I turn back to Fabrice and José. I order a double espresso in my husky ex-smoker's voice.

"Are you making sketches?" I ask her.

"You're very observant."

It takes me a few seconds to grasp the irony of her reply, softened by the smile that has just lit up her features.

"I'm sketching this and that, yes. I like coming here in the morning. And sometimes part of the afternoon. I like the atmosphere."

"It's too quiet. Apparently it does good business in the evening."

"I don't come in the evening."

"Do you work at night?"

She laughs this time. She laughs without putting her hands in front of her mouth, and I appreciate the frankness of her reaction.

"No, I'm not working at the moment. I came back at the start of lockdown, and I've been holed up here ever since. Last summer I worked as a checkout attendant, but they didn't renew my contract. I'm staying at my mother's place, and she lives in the south with her . . . I'm sorry, I don't know why I'm telling you all this."

"Because I asked you?"

"No. You just wanted to know if I worked at night."

"Let's just say your answer was very thorough."

Her smile, again. She's one of those people whose face changes radically the minute they smile, and the pleasure is contagious. There's a pause in our conversation, which is not yet really a conversation, and neither one of us feels awkward. It's like sitting in the grass, in the shade, after a long trek under the sun. I ask her if I can remove my mask, since I'm vaccinated. She nods her head. I start chattering again. Nothing better than a confession to arouse interest.

"I used to run this café, before."

She doesn't exclaim. She registers the information calmly, blinking twice. She asks me if I'm nostalgic for those days.

"Not at all. For the café I ran a long time ago, The Atlantic, maybe, yes. But this place, no. I never really felt at home here. And besides, customers know how to make real nuisances of themselves. It was very different before, you know. We didn't offer hot food. On the other hand we sold the local papers. The new boss didn't want to bother with all that."

"Who? Fabrice?"

I recoil, almost imperceptibly, but she catches it. It's undeniable, she's observant. She stores up details and maybe she commits them to one of those notebooks she carries around with her. I wonder what her drawings are like. She hastily closed her sketchbook when I intruded. It could well be she was in the middle of sketching my portrait.

"Do you know him?"

She shakes her head. She replies that they were in the same class in middle school, but apparently he doesn't remember her at all. But she remembers him. Not because he was particularly handsome or intelligent, or the opposite, for that matter. Simply, he'd helped her grasp some notion of mathematics she was struggling with. It had brightened her day. They're rare, aren't they, people who brighten your day? I remain pensive. Lowering my voice, I tell her that Fabrice also brightened one of my days, several days in a row, even. I tell her about our week on the coast. How he didn't interfere during that time. That's even rarer, isn't it, someone who knows when not to interfere?

She glances over at the bar. Fabrice is preparing a platter for a group that has just sat down out on the terrace. José has gone into the kitchen to help Ifemelu, the young woman who takes care of lunchtime meals.

When the pandemic struck I was afraid that Fabrice would give up on the whole idea. When he told me José had moved in with him and that they were going to use the slack period to do renovations, I knew it would work out. He's often spoken to me about José—even though José himself doesn't know. Brothers. That's what they look like when you see them working together. But José could never brighten my days, because he hasn't got a clue, how not to interfere. He's all about projection. Into the future. Elsewhere. I wonder how much longer he'll stay. You can sense the impatience In his hands and legs. He dreams of getting out and the lockdown can't have improved things.

I Half rest. When I was little, I dreamed of learning to play the piano, but my parents didn't have the means to pay for lessons. I asked a classmate to teach me the basics about the notes and I practiced on a keyboard I made of cardboard. She's the one who taught me about phrasing. Pause. Half rest. Half note. Quarter note rest. I realize I've just joined the melodic line of the young woman sitting across from me. When I start speaking again, we're in harmony. She won't sidestep the questions anymore.

"Where was it you came back from?"

"I'm sorry?"

"You said earlier that you came back at the beginning of lockdown. You weren't in the south with your mother. So, west, east, or north?"

"North. The far north."

"Iceland?"

"Farther east."

I unfold the map in my mind. The Scandinavian countries. I always used to mix up Sweden and Norway. She doesn't leave me the time to suggest a name. She slumps a little and explains that she lived in Finland. Yes, the country of reindeer and Father Christmas. Also the country of crazy writers and filmmakers, she adds. I'm trying to remember the capital. I murmur, "You were in Helsinki?" And add a question mark at the end of the sentence.

"Almost. Vantaa. Just outside."

"And, forgive my indiscretion, but what compels a young woman to go and live in a Nordic country? Love?"

"No, not at first. Work. And connections are what make you stay, of course. I thought I'd spend my life there. Even at the lycée, when the others talked about nothing but beaches and suntans, I pictured myself in an igloo or walking through huge forests of snow-covered pine trees."

"And did you fulfill your dream?"

"The igloo, no. But the walking, yes."

"What were you doing there?"

She takes a deep breath.

"Are you sure you want to know? It's a very long story! And so dreary, you can't imagine."

"Are you trying to get rid of me? You're out of luck, I think I'll grab the menu and order lunch. I'm hungry, aren't you?"

CHLOÉ

THIS IS JUST what I've been waiting for, actually. For someone to come and disturb me. Unsettle me. Stop me from going on with my sketches. Interrupt my train of thought. This constant tendency to let myself be governed by events. Deciding nothing on my own. It's annoying. I know I have to change. I've been telling myself the same thing every day since I got back.

I remember that hour of class. The English teacher, Madame Léautaud—sorry, Mrs. Lee ooh-too, was what she wanted us to call her—told us to think of a destination for our next vacation, to imagine that we had an unlimited budget, and then justify our choice in two or three hundred words. My friends had all chosen sunshine and beach parties on the shores of the Mediterranean or the Atlantic. The more adventurous students, or the bootlickers, had held forth about the United States and their terribly original desire to see New York, the Statue of Liberty, and the Empire State Building, along with a musical on Broadway. A certain Céline, who had a pierced nostril, had turned her nose up at the others with her determination to save the planet, and thus make the most of the time offered to her to work with a humanitarian association in India. And what about you, Chloé? Where would you like to go?

I'd prepared only a few notes. I didn't feel inspired. I talked about Denmark and Sweden, and my fear of hot weather, of torrid summers and being obliged to smear myself with special high-protection sunscreen for baby skin, to be sure I wouldn't come home looking like a lobster. So, burning on the sand was really not my thing. I'd rather take a trip to the Arctic Circle to meet descendants of the Vikings. I'd seen a news story about Copenhagen where we learned that it was the city with the happiest people on earth. Or at least that was what had emerged from surveys, so I was intrigued. I really wanted to see happy folk, instead of these people who were forever sulking and complaining.

After I'd finished, you could have knocked Mrs. Lee-ooh-too down with a feather. It was the first time I'd actually spoken at any length, and she could see my English actually wasn't half bad. She repeated the word "interesting" several times, and even concluded with a "fascinating"—and then she asked Souleymane for his presentation, and he came out with just the opposite sort of thing—how attached he was to his country of origin and how he wanted to go there and see it, again, in all its colors, and above all, how he would like to feel less excluded than he did here, among all these pale faces. Souleymane had a real sense of humor, and my frozen Nanook of the North side was no match for his warmth. No one mentioned my little speech after class.

After that, I didn't give it any serious thought. Like most of the students I allowed myself to go with the flow, depending on my grades and the teachers' verdicts. I was seen as a discreet, serious young woman, with little enthusiasm for science, and nearly all the teachers agreed I should be steered toward accountancy or law, two subjects that general education teachers hardly knew anything about. I say "nearly all" only because at one point Mrs. Lee-ooh-too had emphasized the fact that I did have an original mind in spite of everything, and had shown myself to be extremely perspicacious. In short, I might be a little weird, but hardly a fundamentally unpleasant person, and I probably ought to find my way somewhere off the beaten path—she could picture me in some import-export business with the Nordic countries. There must have been some stifled laughter at student-faculty meetings, but the notion of import-export stuck, as did my drawing abilities, which had been spotted more than once during class, where I spent my time filling the pages of my binders with things that were definitely not handwritten.

After the baccalaureate exam, I enrolled at university in Paris, in a sort of catch-all faculty where they offered classes in the mastery of new communications networks, as well as graphic design, marketing, and an entire range of foreign languages—I chose Swedish because over the last few years I'd learned the basics on the Internet. I knew certain turns of phrase, the most common tenses, short answers, the essential grammar rules—the lecturer was very impressed and he must have told others around him about me. At the end of the third year I was offered an internship during the university vacation—in Malmö, at the southern end of Sweden. I would receive a small stipend but I also had room and board, which in Scandinavian countries was a luxury. I'd been single for nearly six months, I hadn't kept in touch with that many of my friends from the lycée, and the ones I'd met in university were very excited about the prospect of coming to visit me. Naturally, I agreed. I never really came back. I finished my studies by means of correspondence courses. In the meantime I worked my way up from a start-up to a major company, from a position as marketing assistant to that of French market specialist, at a time when my compatriots were beginning to show an interest in environmental protection. I surfed on the green wave of all things natural and organic. And most important of all, I met Ari.

Ari was in Malmö on a six-month contract only, on loan from his parent company, which was located on the other side of the border, in Finland, that rather strange country where no one ever went, and whose language was like no other. Ari developed applications whose aim was to gather ever-increasing amounts of consumer data—people's habits and preferences. In the evening he would play beautifully on his acoustic guitar, traditional ballads and Anglo-Saxon classics. In his living room all the space was taken up by four sofas set out in a square, where the two of us—and anyone else who felt like it—could sit and read. Ari was very sociable and had a lot of friends. I slipped easily into his life. I moved to a new house and the company I was working for in

Sweden transferred me to its Finnish branch. Weeks went by. Months. A year, then two. Time could stretch to infinity. I'd found my place in the world. Except professionally: it wasn't my vocation, this working in open-plan offices, or any office, for that matter. We gave it some thought, Ari and I. He was the one who came up with the idea of a tearoom. After all, I spent a lot of time cooking whenever we had guests, because they were always eager to try food from abroad. I had collected a pile of recipes and would try them out, focusing on desserts.

I shrugged. Told him I'd think about it. At night, the idea began to obsess me in my dreams. A month later I told my boss I was going to embark on something new. He encouraged me. In Scandinavia they want their workers to feel fulfilled, and he'd noticed that I'd seemed frustrated lately. I mentioned my project to him. He promised to be one of my first customers. He kept his word. He came all the way to Vantaa.

I can still hear the sound of it all. *Anteeksi, en puhu suomea. Puhutteko englantia?* That language that remains impenetrable, even to their Nordic neighbors. That language I was still struggling with, years after I'd moved there. I resorted to Swedish and above all English—everyone speaks English in Finland, and Swedish is the second official language. I read that a former Finnish minister of foreign affairs had wanted English to become the third official language, in order to attract foreign investors and workers. French became a refuge in my dreams. There was surely information I didn't get, details I missed. The locals have a tendency to revert to their own idiom when the situation gets complicated or they become intimate. I might have realized what was going to happen. I would have been better prepared. But it's pointless to have regrets. I'm here now, sitting across from this woman who's just told me her name—Jocelyne, one of those names that has totally disappeared and that immediately makes you think of the postwar years and the 1950s. This woman used to run a café, like me.

I had a tearoom in Vantaa, Finland. That sounds like the beginning of a memoir by Karen Blixen. When I murmur those words it all comes back. The most infinitesimal details, the tiny carvings in the wooden tables, the sound of the coffee machine, the color of the cappuccino Mrs. Kalmus liked to drink, telling me each time about her childhood in Estonia, near Tartu, the lakes where she used to swim with her brothers; there's roughly one lake per family in Estonia, she assured me. Ilona, who helped me out on a regular basis and whom I compensated however I could—I wasn't sound enough financially yet to hire her outright. The Jassim family, from Syria, who would exchange a few words with me every day, and joke about the fact we were uprooted, all of us. Except that they really had trouble with the climate. Most of the Iraqis who'd immigrated the previous year requested to return home. They couldn't adapt. But not the Syrians. They knew they couldn't go home, that they had to get used to the cold and the endless winter nights, whatever the cost.

Talking. That's probably what I miss most. All those unfinished drafts of conversations. All those people who came and left some of their sorrow or joy, and who wanted nothing more than to be listened to. I played that role. It's strange, now, to find myself on the other side of the mirror. In the role of the antisocial customer, who takes up a table all day long. There weren't many like that in my tearoom. It was too expensive. Too French. Too classy. I think that, unlike José, it wouldn't have bothered me.

What I don't miss is the cooking. I couldn't take it anymore. I was about to hire Ilona to help out, or even replace me, in the kitchen, to have her make the cakes and pies according to my recipes. But I loved the place. Deeply. Even if it was on the ground floor of a charmless four-story building, surrounded by other charmless four-story buildings, and it gave onto a concrete square with a few flower tubs and two or three benches. I could easily see myself getting old there, with Ari by my side. He was the one who took care of the lease and the insurance. I simply signed on the line. Children? We were hesitating because of climate change and the world spiraling downward. Summers in Finland were hot now, and people looked at the sky as if it represented a threat. They'd never seen anything like it before. Ari was in no hurry, either. He wanted to prolong the carefree life of a young man, which suited him so perfectly. No strings. No home port—although in fact he was the one who had come back to drop anchor where he'd sailed from.

I think my desire for motherhood only kicked in when I met Annika. She came to look after Ari's sister, Helena, who was pregnant, but her pregnancy wasn't going the way she'd imagined. She had dreamed of three trimesters of blooming and plenitude, but her body rebelled: She felt nauseous all the time, had difficulty walking for longer than fifteen minutes, and often complained of pain in her belly, even though the medical exams hadn't found anything abnormal. It was probably stress. The fear of giving birth and its consequences. The life change brought on by the arrival of a baby. I would observe Helena and everything seemed to confirm my own rejection of motherhood. And then she decided to contact a doula, Annika.

I was there when they met for the first time. I had stopped by with some apple pie and a smoothie for Helena—the apartment she shared with her husband was not far from the tearoom and my intention was to make peace with Helena. Our relationship had not always been easy. She preferred her brother's previous fiancée, who was one of her childhood friends, and she initially gave me a rather chilly reception. Once she was pregnant things between us changed somewhat. She needed support. I was ready to help her, even if the doula would surely know better than I what needed to be done.

Doula. Nobody in France knows the full significance of the word. It's a concept born in the US. A doula is someone who is paid to accompany mothers-to-be or couples during pregnancy. She doesn't play a medical role. She cannot administer medication or write prescriptions. She's there to ensure the smooth trajectory of the pregnancy, and she sees to the future mother's well-being by giving her advice and massages and listening attentively to everything she says, while preparing her herbal tea and the right sort of meals. I was curious to see what this doula would recommend for Helena on a nutritional level. I asked her if I could stay for their first meeting, or whether she'd rather I make myself scarce. Helena hesitated half a second before agreeing. Annika immediately picked up on her reluctance, and she smiled and said that she and I would be more comfortable chatting in the ambience of my tearoom. *You have a tearoom in Simonkylä, don't you?*

I felt myself blushing as I nodded. I really wished I could be like Annika. Warm, attractive, and sure of herself. I got ready to leave the apartment, while they began talking about the unborn child, what it could be experiencing, the pleasure it might feel when the mother was relaxed and happy. Annika had had two children early on with her partner. They'd separated three years ago, in the most gentle manner. No one had been hurt. In any case, we aren't on earth to suffer. That was the last thing I heard. They followed me down the stairs. Outside, night was already falling.

JOCELYNE

"CAN I CLEAR this away for you?"

I am so immersed in the young woman's story that José's interruption startles me. He doesn't wait for an answer but imposes his presence, piling the empty plates onto his tray. I realize that I have only the vaguest memory of the actual lunch—I ate the croque-madame without noticing, absorbed as I was in Chloé's story.

"Can I get you some coffee?"

Chloé has snapped shut like a clam and is staring at the fountain out on the square. She's beyond reach now.

"Yes. For both of us. And the bill, please. That way you won't need to disturb us again. Particularly when we didn't ask for anything."

José goes off in a huff, back behind the bar, incensed. He clatters glasses and plates to make it clear to us he is not pleased. Chloé still hasn't said anything. I ask her to excuse me for a few minutes—I'll be right back. I head to the bar, with my most confident step, and I sit on one of the stools. José is so surprised that for a moment he falters. He's not used to people resisting him.

"Do you know who I am, José?"

"Absolutely no idea."

"Fabrice never told you about me?"

He stands stock-still and frowns.

"You're not his mother. I've already met her. And almost his entire family."

"I know. You've been partners since childhood."

"*Partners?*"

"That would be the right word, don't you think? 'Friends' would put both of you ill at ease. And yet, you may be the person who knows him best of all. You lived together during lockdown, didn't you?"

"But how do you—"

"Stop mumbling and listen to me. I know that you look out for him and that's all to your credit. So do I, after a fashion. I'm the former owner of this place. I ran it for over ten years. And before that I ran another café on the Boulevard du 14 Juillet. The Atlantic. Quite an adventure."

José gives a faint smile.

"I remember that place. I wasn't a customer. I went to the other side of town. Near the technical high school."

"Chez Mous'?"

All of a sudden his face lights up. He's fifteen years old, he's drinking beer with his pals. He's making fun of his teachers. He hopes he'll find a job soon, because he wants his financial independence, to get away from the restricted life his parents lead. Waiter. At Chez Mous'. That would be ideal, for a first go. But Mous' doesn't need anyone. Mous' doesn't let others do things in his place.

"I loved that place."

"I can well imagine. The proprietor, on the other hand, was a real bastard."

He bursts out laughing and shakes his head.

"You don't mince your words!"

"No, I like them whole. Besides, the advantage of getting old is that you can say what you want. In any case, José, honestly, don't go getting annoyed with me or with that girl. We're not your enemies. And we aren't parasites."

He picks up some clean cups, to wash them again. We let a few seconds go by. The words I've just said mingle with the scent of liquid soap.

"Right. So you'll look after him?"

"Sorry?"

"I'll be leaving him . . . I mean, I'm going to leave soon."

All at once we're in a bubble, the two of us. The decor fades away and we stare at each other without hostility. I notice his jaws are clenched. José is a sentimental man. José has grown attached. José is afraid of hurting people. When he feels guilty, he takes it out on others. I slide my hand over the counter and touch his cheek. The world seems to stop turning for a moment.

"I suppose you haven't said anything to him yet?" I ask.

"I don't dare."

"It won't kill him. I'm sure he'll be sad, but it won't kill him."

"In fact, I think what scares me the most is that he might not care one way or the other."

"That's impossible and you know it, José."

"But I'm not abandoning him, huh. I'll stay in touch, of course I will. I'll go back on social networks, if I have to. And I'll write him letters."

His words are suspended in the air for a moment, and I picture José bent over a sheet of paper, writing sentences in an era where messages are rarely longer than a dozen words. There's nothing ridiculous about it, on the contrary. It's very touching. I can't remember the last time I got a real letter—anything besides bills and flyers.

"You're very fond of him, aren't you?"

He lowers his eyes. Holds a glass up to the light, looking for suspicious streaks. Tilts his head. End of discussion.

"In any case, Chloé and I would like some coffee. Out on the terrace, rather, now that the sun has come out. A glass of rosé, too, for me. We have something to celebrate . . ."

"My departure?"

"Yes, why not, after all? Your new departure. And the kid's arrival."

"She's not that young. They were in class together."

"That's what I'm saying. Fabrice is a kid, too. He's my kid."

"Have you seen what she's drawing?"

"Not really, no."

"It's really good. Well, I don't know anything about art. But it's . . . It's full of life. Oh, and thank you."

"For what?"

"I don't really know."

I go back and tell Chloé that we're moving out onto the terrace. It's starting to get crowded out there. Fabrice is running left and right, and drops of sweat are beading on his brow. Ifemelu in the kitchen is getting irritated, regularly ringing the bell to signal that the orders are ready. Just like at Chez Mous', fifteen years ago. I hold back a smile at the thought of his name. *Mous'*. A reference to the head on a glass of beer, or so we thought. *Mousse*. Short for *Moustache*, he proclaimed, showing off his whiskers. Nobody would have dreamed that in fact it was a diminutive of his real first name, Mustafa. I love hidden meanings. I love the thought that people come to Le Tom's without knowing what the name stands for.

Mous'. I can still see his face in the half-light of the big room. I wonder if anyone knows the actual circumstances of his death. Not his widow, in any case, and it's better that way. Mous' died of a heart attack in the mountains while he was busy servicing a lady who wasn't his wife. A good death, no? Mous' was a tireless womanizer. I'm sure that if I concentrate for a moment, I can recall the sensation, the weight of his body on mine, and the ridiculous little whimper that preceded his orgasm.

I stare at the spot just past Chloé's shoulder and smile. Chloé gives a little frown. She asks me what I'm thinking about. When I reply, "About sex," she says she's not the least bit surprised.

"Tell me, instead, some more about Annika," I say. "That's where we left off, isn't it?"

CHLOÉ—ON THE TERRACE

ANNIKA AND I hit it off right away. She came to the tearoom two days later and we chatted as if we'd known each other for years. We spoke Swedish together right from the start—it was her suggestion. Her mother was from Stockholm and Annika spoke a fluid Swedish that reminded me of my classes at university. It was a subtle way of making me feel Scandinavian, without resorting to Finnish, which was often still opaque to me. She talked at length about her profession as a doula, even though she drew the line at going into details about the couples she'd been helping, particularly Helena and her husband. She was fascinated by what was proving to be a profession at the crossroads between medicine and psychology. When I asked her, quite naively, whether I could be a doula, she burst out laughing, then apologized. She said that there was no reason why not, in practice, because the legal status of the profession was still a bit vague, but it was nevertheless highly recommended for a practitioner to have already had their own experience of motherhood. Not to mention fluency in the local language. She glanced around the room and smiled: "But why would you ever want to leave this place? It's fantastic, isn't it, to have your own business, giving pleasure to people? That's absolutely vital in life." Give pleasure. The expression was not part of my everyday vocabulary. Ari complained gently about my lack of inventiveness and what he termed my sexual timidity, although I would have used the word "modesty." Maybe Annika would have some advice for me, when we got to know each other better?

When the premises next to the tearoom became vacant, I let her know at once. I knew she'd been looking for a professional space for all the administrative tasks, and for meeting with expectant mothers outside their home from time to time. She would furnish it with deep couches and create an atmosphere conducive to meditation or intimate conversation. The ideal thing, she said, would be a little apartment, not too expensive, but cozy. The one I suggested suited her perfectly. She was enchanted. We even celebrated in my tearoom with fake Russian champagne. She told me about her first loves. She'd had multiple experiences, very young. She was neither ashamed nor proud of the fact. She thought that we all had different paths in life, and this was what made each encounter so enriching. As for Annika herself, she liked people's skin. The taste of it. She would have liked to be able to collect the smell of each of her lovers. She would have loved to be a nose for a perfumer.

I'd reached this point in the story when Fabrice came and stood by our table with our coffees and asked if he could join us for a few minutes. Jocelyne frowned and said that, in fact, his timing was not great, but oh well, how could she refuse him anything. He murmured a few words in apology, as his neck began to flush crimson, and he was about to walk away when Jocelyne barked, "Sit down!," startling the patrons at the other tables.

Fabrice's presence muddled my thoughts. I had difficulty concentrating and I couldn't pick up the thread of my memories. I mumbled a few words to start a sentence, but I no longer felt like talking. Jocelyne lectured Fabrice, "You don't interrupt a private conversation, that's all there is to it. You wait until you're invited—it's a courtesy, pure and simple, for Christ's sake. Basic manners. In the meantime, look what you've done," she added, turning toward me, "She's lost. You were in the middle of talking about Annika and the professional space she rented next to your café." I corrected her and said it was actually a tearoom. We didn't serve alcohol. We would probably have done better business, but I didn't want to deal with drunken customers. The Finns drink a lot of beer, and behave like everyone else the minute they've had one too many. Fabrice couldn't help but interrupt again, which triggered Jocelyne's anger.

"Oh wow, you're in the business, then? You could . . . No, never mind."

I think we all finished his sentence mentally, but none of us finished it out loud. Fabrice, because he realized he'd gone too far and knew nothing about me; Jocelyne because she found his reaction totally inappropriate. We were examining my past, not my future. And I didn't finish his sentence because I didn't feel like moving. Didn't feel like going from observation to action. I'd already had enough trouble extricating myself from my family home and dragging myself this far. Every morning was a new victory. An escape from the quicksand of my mother's house. I was making my way back toward life. I managed to get myself out once already, last summer, after a terrible struggle against apathy, to work at the little local supermarket. They were looking for someone for the checkout and to stack shelves. They didn't expect to find someone as qualified as I am. They were delighted and they asked me to stay on that autumn but I was just beginning to emerge from my half-slumber and to look further ahead, so I declined their offer, convinced I'd be able to channel my energy and find work that would better correspond to my expectations.

And then came the first curfew, followed not long after by the second and the third, which required everyone to be at home in the evening by six o'clock sharp, which meant that we were all rushing through the streets to make it, as if some mortal disease were hot on our heels. There were fewer job offers now. I became a recluse again. In the house I went around in circles for hours on end, day and night. I know every nook and cranny. More than six months of restless wandering in an enclosed space. At one point I thought I'd be imprisoned forever among those furnishings I hadn't even chosen. My mother thought so too, for that matter. She began to worry. She would call, and find me confused. At the beginning of spring she asked a neighbor to come and make sure I was taking good care of the place. I acted charming

for the length of the visit, because I figured it had been mas-
terminded from a distance. I pretended to be eager for any
gardening advice. I emphasized how long it was taking me to
look after that house that was too big for me. He called my
mother to reassure her; everything was under control.

Nevertheless, she announced that she thought she'd
come back for a while in August this year when the heat gets
unbearable in the Southeast. She didn't know yet whether
she'd come on her own. She needed to talk to me, to get
to the bottom of what happened to me, and how I saw my
future. The threat of her sudden appearance in my world
had the advantage of shaking me out of my torpor. I had to
go back into the world—but I could only make that return
voyage progressively. In stages. First I had to find a refuge
where I could observe my fellow humans. Initially I thought
of the multimedia library—but the regular users were lon-
ers like me. Temporarily excluded. A café—yes. Not a tearoom—in France, the few remaining tearooms cater only
to a very select clientele. A café. A popular place. Set back
slightly from the commotion of the center of town, but in
a street with plenty of foot traffic all the same. On my first
outing, I kept blinking all the time, as if I'd been immersed
in darkness for a very long time and the light was blinding.
A mole—that's what I'd become. Not an old woman. A rela-
tively young one. But a little battered. Who'd want anything
to do with a battered mole?

"Why don't we resume our conversation a little later, all
right, Chloé? I have an appointment at three o'clock, but

I'll come back here this evening. For the aperitif. Here's my number. Call me and that way I'll have yours. Fabrice, I'd like the bill, if it's no bother."

Fabrice hesitates for a few seconds. I get the impression he'd like to hear more about the battered mole, but he complies. Fabrice is not a rebel. I've grasped that much from observing him. He maneuvers between other people's orders and his own desires. He's trying to stay on course. From time to time, like just now, he gets frustrated. There's a line across his forehead. I can't help but smile. He's risen to the bait. I hardly dared to hope for as much.

3:00 P.M.

JOSÉ

WE REALLY NEED to hire someone to help Ifemelu in the kitchen, otherwise we won't manage. Well, *Fabrice* won't manage. I rephrase what I just said and make a face. I'm going to have trouble letting go, and I hate this feeling of dependency. Freedom of movement is what I want more than anything—particularly after eighteen months of restrictions.

Customers are returning. I'm relieved. Even last year we did well in July and August—but people would only sit out on the terrace, keeping their distance and often wearing their mask. They were being cautious, timid. Nobody ventured inside. It had become taboo. They stayed outside and took photos of each other to show on Snapchat how they'd come back to life. How things were back to normal. It lasted a few weeks. I don't know what's going to happen this year. I have my doubts. I heard this morning that the United Kingdom was adopting some sort of Covid passport. You can cross the channel now only if you've been double vaccinated—and that doesn't mean you won't have to go into quarantine when you get there. As soon as the borders lower their guard, I'll get the hell out. Ann and Peter are waiting for me in Scotland.

I met them here a couple of years ago. They told me about their alternative farming project. Before they left they said they could always use an extra pair of hands. That will be my first port of call.

I told him.

Just now, a little earlier. It was just the two of us. The woman with the drawings—Chloé, that is, since that's her name—left shortly after the previous owner of the café did. Fabrice was biting his nails. In the beginning I thought it wasn't the right time, because something else was bugging him: how to get that girl's attention, and how to make the best impression. And then in the end I understood that maybe that wasn't a bad thing. As long as he was imagining a potential liaison, it would come as less of a blow. The news of my departure wouldn't take up all the space.

He took it in his stride. I know him inside out. He looked away so that I couldn't see how he felt. He got busy, and justified it saying that he'd just heard some thunder, that the rain was on its way back and we'd have to take down the umbrellas right away. Never mind the tables and chairs, we could wipe them down later. I let him get on with it. I know he needs a certain amount of time to digest this kind of news. Later, he slumped onto the banquette at table number four. I was behind the counter washing glasses for the umpteenth time, trying to appear composed. He motioned to me to come over. I readied myself for an onslaught of insults or a series of questions—how, for who, why, was it because of the salary, the working conditions, the responsibilities? I also expected some emotional blackmail, references to our adolescence, our cohabitation, all the welter of things we've shared and that connect us. He didn't bring up any of that. He didn't open his mouth. I could sense the words caught in his throat that couldn't find their way out. I felt bad for him. I tried to help him. I wanted to start speaking, but just as I was about to, he made this incredible gesture: he placed his forefinger on my lips and murmured that he'd miss me a lot.

I saw the bypass that separated our neighborhoods. The confrontation with the three scumbags. Our morning jogs through the park. I said I'd miss him, too, and I looked deep in his eyes. It was one of the most disturbing moments of my life. I don't think I've ever been that close to anyone before. Then I tore myself away. Even though it was the beginning of the afternoon and customers would probably be filling the terrace before long, once the shower ended, I went and got a glass of very peaty Scotch whiskey for me and a beer with a touch of lime and sparkling water for him. I often made fun of his penchant for this drink, something for well-mannered young Englishwomen—lager and lime; it's refreshing and won't make you drunk at all. I explained things to him. My need to escape, exacerbated by the weeks of confinement and the various curfews. I'd be living from day to day, but it would be a life of my own choosing, not one imposed on me. He smiled and said that it was astonishing nonetheless, in the middle of the pandemic. I shrugged. I was one of the first in my age group to have gotten vaccinated—I figured that the borders would stay closed to people who refused to get the jab.

"I knew you were a gypsy at heart."

Those were his words, later. He added that he liked the idea, and how it contrasted with the image I projected—this insular guy, borderline sinister-looking. A product of the high-rise apartment blocks on the other side of the bypass, still a prisoner of his background despite his lodgings in the center of town. I shook my head when he used that word, "sinister." That's one of the things that appealed to me about him right from the start. His way with words. How he can run circles around the people he's speaking to.

He closed his eyes. He said that there were contrasts between us, too. He was a man of the indoors. He liked this room, the banquettes—yes, the leatherette was unpleasant, but never mind—the music in the background, the wooden bar counter. I was always drawn to the terrace, to the sunshine and wind—outdoors. He'd been to London once, and Madrid, too, but he didn't feel the urge to trek around the planet and gorge himself with people and places. He was putting down roots. Maybe he was getting set in his ways. It didn't matter. It was here and now that he felt good.

I spoke about my replacement. He sighed. I went on to specify that I'd given it a lot of thought, even though it might not look that way, and that I'd found just the right person, but I didn't know if he, Fabrice, would go along with it. I even thought he would refuse outright.

"Why is that?"

"His name is Ahmed."

"So? May I remind you I hired Ifemelu and that—"

"He's one of the three guys you gave the money to, to pay off my debts."

I'd expected anything but his peals of laughter. Spontaneous. Loud. Uncontrollable. He was shaking so hard, gasping, that he had to go and calm down in the restroom and splash his face with water. When he came back, he was beaming.

"You mean that all this time you stayed friends with the guys who wanted to smash your face in?"

"For a start, I'm not sure they would have. And then, they were right. I was the one who fucked up, not them. In the beginning we avoided each other. They made fun of me and my protector, but the following summer I got Ahmed out of a tight spot and after that, the slate was clean."

"So your Ahmed who extorts money wants to work like a dog for a crap salary. Really?"

"For a start, it's up to you to see that the salary is appropriate, and then, wait till you've tasted his cooking before you judge him."

"His favorite dishes?"

"Complicated salads. Vegetarian lasagna. A winter squash pie—he won't give me the recipe. He hasn't eaten meat for years."

"And is he a clandestine member of Greenpeace, as well?"

"Why? Is that incompatible with the fact his name is Ahmed?"

Fabrice lowered his gaze—I knew I'd struck home. An easy target. All of us, in some recess in our brain, have racist or sexist stereotypes just waiting to sneak out in the middle of a hasty reply. All of us. The important thing is just to be aware of it—and to apologize afterward. Fabrice raised both hands in a sign of surrender, and I couldn't help but drive the point home.

"By the way, Ahmed's family has been living here since the early twentieth century. They've lost count of how many generations. He'll go well with your Finnish friend. To resort to the clichés: hot and cold. Fire and ice."

There was a sudden moment of silence. Not a single car went by in the street. Not a soul anywhere. We could have been the last survivors of a cataclysm. Fabrice narrowed his eyes.

"My Finnish friend?"

"The girl who stays here all morning drawing."

"Her name is Chloé."

"I know. I keep my ears open. I heard her tell the old woman that she had a tearoom in Finland."

"The old woman has a name, it's Jocelyne."

"Yes, she told me. She also mentioned that you two were connected. Which just goes to show, you don't tell me everything. That's probably what made me decide to confess everything today. In the end, we're even. You never told me about her, and I never said anything about my urge to go away."

"It's not a fight, José. We're not in a competition."

We stayed for a few moments in silence. Outside, a sudden shower had drenched the town, stopping as abruptly as it had started. I thought about the monsoon. I wondered when, in my round-the-world tour, I would pass through India. When there would be no more variants. When we would have forgotten the very term itself, "variants." I would drink an insipid beer in a bar in New Delhi or Mumbai and I'd have a thought for Fabrice and his Finnish friend, who'd be cleaning and tidying up at Le Tom's. I started speaking again.

"Fabrice, you know, you really ought to change the name of this place. It's . . . It sounds like something out of the '70s. It doesn't represent what we've done here. What the café's become."

"I can't change it."

"What do you mean, you can't change it?"

"I promised. I keep my promises."

He stood up, stretched, and opened the door wide. The sun was slipping through the clouds. There still weren't many people going by, but in a while the customers would return. Particularly once the offices closed for the day. They're so happy to be gradually getting back into their old habits. An aperitif. Or two. A few dubious jokes. After a few minutes the conversation will shift to the boss, or a colleague who, worse luck, doesn't fit the mold. There's always some girl who'll come to their defense, who'll say that you have to respect everyone's opinion, so they change the subject again, go on to discuss how the local soccer team's doing, or their vacations. The ones they've been fantasizing about, that they'll spend in the Dominican Republic, in Croatia, or in Miami in a four-star hotel, where they'll sit by the pool sipping cocktails all the livelong day. And their real vacations: one week at our grandparents' place, we would've liked to leave the kid with them, but they're going trekking somewhere, it's a nuisance, you can never count on them. And then two weeks in Mimizan camping with friends. The campsite's a little far from the ocean but we'll rent bikes. And when we come home, we'll meet up here and share all our stories, how does that sound?

I'll be long gone. I won't here to admire their fucking suntans this year. I won't hear their pathetic anecdotes. I'll be miles away. Moors as far as the eye can see. Sheep bleating. The cool air, rain on the heather. I won't miss any of it. Or anyone. Except Fabrice.

He's the only one I'll miss.

MANON, 42—ON THE TERRACE

THE FIRST person I see. I can't believe it. No, honestly, what were the odds, out of ten thousand, say, for this to happen? And "odds" is not the right word. Bad luck, rather.

I felt like getting some fresh air. It was still early. I hadn't planned to stop off at a café, or even to go shopping. I just wanted to walk around, get back into my old routine. For the last few weeks now, it's been okay to go where you want, for as long as you want, but my body still seems to be in lockdown, respecting curfews—well, limiting social contact, in a way. I have to domesticate it, teach it all over again what the outdoors is, what personal interaction is—feelings, too. I suppose I'm not the only one: a whole host of individuals became recluses and are finding it difficult to open up again.

I instantly sensed that I might find myself falling back into my bad habits. Into solitude, isolation, and a sort of shame. Whereas at the beginning, I fought it. I went to virtual cocktail parties, flitted from one social network to the next, and I tried to keep in touch with everyone I knew. And then, like everyone, I got bored with it. I wanted living

people. Blood. Flesh. Skin. It was time to get out again.
And then I go and run into him, and everything skids off
the rails.

To be perfectly honest, I suspected he might be around.
I saw the obituary for his father, and that's the sort of event
you cannot get out of, even if you live on the other side of
the planet. I'll be confronted with it, too, in the years to
come, since my parents are pushing eighty, but I'd rather
not think about it. For the time being they're in great shape.
They have a lot of plans. When I have lunch with them,
they speak volubly about everything they're going to do in
the months to come, and the trips they still dream of taking. Naturally, the virus has put a damper on their enthusiasm, but now that they're vaccinated they've started leafing
through the travel brochures again. Their only concern, in
fact, even if they don't show it, is me. My celibacy. For a
long time my father tried to find out by any means possible
whether I was "seeing someone." He really persisted—man
or woman, he didn't care, as long as I was happy. My father
cannot conceive of a person being happy on their own. He's
right. We can't be.

I'm not going to complain, though—part of it is my own
fault. I'm not prepared to put up with anything no matter
what simply to be in a duo, and I'm hardly the greatest advo-
cate for coupledom. I have found self-fulfillment through my
profession. I love my job at the association, helping migrants
to integrate. It serves a purpose, and what I'm doing there is
useful: Every day I'm confronted with precarious situations

and, unlike most of the people who live in this country, I know what poverty is. I bring relief—and that is probably the most beautiful expression anyone can use in this life.

I see that I'm standing up for myself. Trying to justify myself. It's pathetic. It's as if I were having a conversation with *him*, and explaining by means of A plus B that, no, absolutely not, I am not that embittered fortysomething woman that people have described to him, pursing their lips—the poor woman, what a sad way to end up.

I feel the anger. How it is boiling over inside me. Metal in a state of fusion. It's something I haven't experienced in a very long time, and it's like the lash of a whip. I'd like to walk for hours and scream under railway bridges. To work off my rage. Part of me is stunned, and, I must confess, disconcerted. The other part is horrified and can't get over the fact that I still end up in this state—that the breach has not healed.

All because of him. Although, frankly, when I saw him I didn't recognize him at first. Seventeen years have gone by (yes, yes, I know, soon to be eighteen, seventeen plus ten months, it's ridiculous to be keeping track like this in a corner of my brain, it speaks volumes about the spite I claim not to feel).

I replay the scene. I was happy because I'd gotten up early and I felt great. I decided to go for a long walk, which might actually lead me to the edge of town. The week before I'd walked for so long that I ended up out in the fields, with those hills on the horizon; I hadn't been there since childhood. It was a strange vision—a sad landscape that had hardly changed despite the years. I was deep in thought. I hadn't even noticed that I'd left the town behind. I was thinking about the list of activities I enjoyed, because I wanted to post it above my computer to remind myself that henceforth my aim in life would be to enjoy myself—and going on long walks was one of the first things that came to mind.

I went down the stairs and outside, glanced at the threatening sky—the weather forecast was for intermittent storms, but I figured I'd find a place to shelter if need be, and besides, I like the rain, I don't even understand how I ever could have wanted to bury myself in a country of deserts when I have a deeply temperate nature. European. To my flesh and bones. I belong to this continent, and I almost forgot it. For a long time I had dreams of being a Jane Austen heroine, trying to dodge the raindrops, laughing impertinently at my suitors' remarks.

I continued down Avenue Anatole-France. Streams of cars went by. Some were headed to the hospital. A few months earlier we thought the medical teams would not withstand the pressure, but in the end the building was still standing and the personnel, too, despite their exhaustion. At work, from one day to the next we were no longer allowed to teach the immigrants to read and write—and the adults we'd been teaching didn't have the necessary computer equipment to keep in touch with us online. We lost a lot of them. Some disappeared. I kept Asbige's bracelet. She'd forgotten it in the room, the last day. I was wearing it when I noticed him on the sidewalk across the street.

How can anyone explain it? I recognized him even when he was a long way away, when he wasn't supposed to be there and I hadn't seen him in years. A hollow feeling in my gut. Between hunger and disgust. And then that pain in my lower back, rising up my spine and spreading through my neck.

I think I murmured, "It can't be," but I'm no longer sure of anything because I was submerged by images, sounds, colors, words, all bursting tumultuously out of every corner of my memory, an incredible cacophony. I stumbled and that's what drew his gaze from across the street, at the very moment I was trying to regain control, telling myself mentally, like a mantra, that it was over, over, over.

He crossed Rue de la Liberté and I saw him coming closer. I should have continued on my way, but I was fascinated by the wound that had just reopened, and I couldn't move an inch. My memory had to skip through decades to adjust to his new appearance. A heavier physique I never thought he'd ever have. He was incredibly nervous when we were together, his hands often trembled, it was touching or annoying depending on the circumstances. And his hair. My god, his hair. You never imagine seeing them bald, those lovers from your youth.

I remember his curls. He cherished and hated them at the same time. He wished they weren't so unruly. They often hid his face. I would feel them on my neck, my breasts, my belly. I suddenly stood up straight, as if I were being attacked by an animal. A dog from the past. And yet he looked perfectly harmless, with his baldness, his flabby cheeks, his soft body. I wished this revenge of time could have brought me satisfaction. But it didn't. You have to have something wrong with you to enjoy reveling in collapse.

He said my name with what was almost a question mark. A request for confirmation. I nodded and he smiled. The years had not altered his smile. It breaks his face in two, and opens the world to you.

"I'm happy to see you. I didn't dare come and visit," he declared, timidly.

I nodded again—what else could I do? Say, Well I'm not happy to see you, asshole, I'm still not, and you're still an asshole? I felt my muscles contract; it was harder to breathe.

"You heard about Papa?"

I relaxed a little. It was inevitable. I'd had good relations with the man who, in the end, did not become my father-in-law. He used to go on and on about the fact that I was far too good for his son, who frequently annoyed him. Too impulsive. Too scattered. "Now you, I can tell you have a goal in life, and that you're forging straight ahead to attain it." It was because of sentences like that, that I didn't go to see him when I ended up back here, my wings clipped. I didn't want to disappoint him. I thought I might run into him one day in the street, in the center of town, but there are people whose path you never cross again, and who die without knowing you were living only a few hundred yards from them.

I nodded. He sighed.

"It wasn't a good funeral."

For the first time I met his gaze. He seemed totally faded. I clearly identified the feeling that flashed through me. It was pity. It disappeared as quickly as it had come, but it left its imprint. He went on speaking, as if to himself.

"There were no restrictions on the number of mourners anymore, but it didn't make any difference, because almost nobody came. The older you get, the fewer friends you have, or witnesses of your life, particularly in Papa's case; when all is said and done, he'd never been very sociable or very family-oriented, as they say. He didn't know how to keep his relationships going."

I winced. Perhaps that was why his father and I had gotten along well. I have very nice colleagues, we get through a lot of solid, serious work together, we know how to cheer one another up, but I don't know whether they look on me as a friend. Probably not. We talk very little about our respective lives. I've noticed I no longer let others get near my private life. And I haven't for seventeen years and ten months, that is. After the breakup, something snapped. A vital coil. A little voice kept telling me that it was, obviously, also my fault, since it hadn't happened to anyone else. Of course people went through breakups every day, sometimes amicably, sometimes violently, and these breakups often left a deep wound. But they were not as devastating. As terrifying. You often hear people say that what doesn't kill you makes you stronger. That is the biggest piece of bullshit I've ever heard. What doesn't kill you, kills you all the same.

There was that phone call, one evening. He said he was very excited and very distraught at the same time. He'd been in Australia for four months already, and he'd promised to come home in April. But here's the thing: He'd been offered a permanent job, one that was extremely interesting and above all very well paid. The downside was that he'd have to stay there in Sydney for at least three or four years. Oh, and there was a corollary: Obviously, he couldn't get any time off, initially. He wouldn't be able to come back at Easter. I didn't bat an eyelash. I said it was no problem. We'd reverse the travel—I'd go to him. Once I was there, we could discuss how we envisaged the next stage. There was a moment of silence. Ever since that moment, I've become extremely attentive, during conversations. I pay more attention to the silences than to the words. It has become my trademark, at work. I know how to detect the secrets of the people I want to help. I help those secrets be born—I'm the midwife of words. Back then, I didn't listen. I didn't hear the reticence. Even when he brought up the price of the ticket and the difficulty of getting a visa. I laughed and said that it sounded like he wasn't happy that I was coming. Obviously he protested. Of course I am. He'd been waiting for so long: Was I sure it wouldn't be a problem at work?

I went right ahead and handed in my notice. Everyone around me told me I was crazy. Why not just ask for an unpaid leave rather than resign? I smiled. I knew I wouldn't be coming back. Off I went, lighthearted. I had a little suitcase with the bare minimum. I'd buy everything else there.

Two people could live comfortably now on Étienne's salary—
and I'd find a job in no time. They said it was easy, out there,
once you had your papers.

Étienne.

That's his name. And it still was, when he was standing
there before me, just now, with his runaway bald spot and
embarrassing stoutness, and his tearful gaze like some sickly
basset hound. He doesn't look like himself anymore—all
that's left, to prove his identity, is his name. I shouldn't say
this, but after the anger and the pity came joy. A pure, sharp
joy. Look what you've become. At last you're as ugly on the
outside as you are on the inside.

The flight from Paris to Sydney was very long and I was
impatient to see him. I fidgeted in my seat before I finally
decided to take the sleeping tablet a friend with a fear of flying had given me. I woke up groggy. I even forgot my hand
luggage and the flight attendant had to come running after
me with it. She was a woman of Asian origin, with long black
hair. Why do such useless details become fixed in the bath of
memory, to emerge intact years later?

It was that Qantas employee I was thinking about, seventeen years later, while Étienne stood there before me, uncer-
tain, a shadow of his former self.

"I wanted to call you."

When, Étienne? Seventeen years ago, these last few days,
or at a point in time somewhere in between? After your
divorce, maybe. All that business about the custody of your
daughter, apparently it really got to you. I don't, for all that,

derive any pleasure from it, even if once or twice I must have flung a, "Serves him right!" at the bathroom mirror; one of those moments when at last we allow ourselves to spit out our venom. I didn't try to find out how you were doing—but I did get some news, all the same. After all, you grew up in this town and your parents still lived here. You nurtured friendships that were all the more loyal, given the fact you were living halfway around the world, and it's easy, actually, to maintain distant ties. We're all very good at making ourselves believe that we're surrounded with friends. And then one day, on an airport runway, we realize how badly we've led ourselves astray.

The last time your name came up, it became clear to me that so much water had passed under the bridge that even the most bitter memories had been submerged. Time is a flood, our lands are polders, and the dykes have given way. It was lunch break, and I was with my colleagues, in the little room that looks onto the Parc des Moulins. The conversation shifted to spicy anecdotes. Shameful behavior. Little humiliations. Anne-Lise, busy with the salade niçoise she'd prepared the night before and stored as usual in a yellow Tupperware, started telling us that she had a story about a truly atrocious end to an affair. One of her girlfriends had told her about this friend, get a load of this . . .

The instant you become the spectator of your own story. When you feel out of place in this strange, misty territory where you are playing the role of protagonist and listener at the same time. Even now, nearly two years later, I don't know what to make of this memory.

This woman left everything to go and be with her guy, who was working somewhere halfway around the world, they had it all planned, how they were going to move in together, how she'd get a job and they'd have a good life together, so she arrives out there, Australia or New Zealand, somewhere like that, in the southern hemisphere, and he's there waiting for her at the airport and he tells her it's all over between them.

The other colleagues, letting out a cry. Their disapproval, encompassing all the men on the planet in a bloc, because basically they're all the same, aren't they? Confident of their rights, incapable of putting themselves in the place of others, zero empathy, it's like my Julien, the other day I told him, You could make an effort when you know I'm coming over, I don't know, do a bit of vacuuming, make dinner instead of ordering pizza, and he comes out and says, aren't I being just a typical woman. What the fuck!

And you, Manon, what do you think?

My colleague turned to me, then went a little pale, thought *Shit, I made a boo-boo*, because how could I have an opinion about men, since I'd been living on my own for years, probably with a cat or two? And I would probably die alone in my apartment and they'd find my body only once the neighbors were bothered by the smell. There was an embarrassing moment that I dismissed with a smile, and I said that I totally shared her point of view, and that was why I preferred to live alone rather than in poor company, and my colleagues vigorously nodded their heads and made some mumbling sounds of approval, while crossing their fingers behind their backs, hoping they'd never end up like me.

I could have corrected her, tattletale Anne-Lise, with her anecdotes. For a start, we hadn't planned anything. And he was waiting for me at the airport. His face barely lit up when he saw me. I rushed into his arms and that was when I felt his reticence. Physically. The reticence I'd forced myself to ignore on the telephone. Skin, muscles, and organs do not lie. He was finding it hard to welcome me. That was when I understood. But I wanted the illusion. I couldn't help it. I was exhausted. I'd left everything. This couldn't be happening.

There are sudden shouts from the next table. A child has just knocked over a bottle of soda. The parents are furious. They look as if they'd like to slap the child, but in public it's just not done. I have no children. I wouldn't have been able to teach them to trust others. I think back on what Étienne came out with just now, in the street. How he said he'd wanted to call me.

"But then I realized I didn't have your number."

Such a ridiculous thing to say. So irrelevant. I burst out laughing. So did he. Then he apologized. Ran his hand over his face. Gave a sigh. Added in one breath that he'd like to see me again. He'd decided not to go back there. *Down under.* Where you meet kangaroos on country roads. Where bush fires are becoming epic. Where the end of the world will begin. Where the end of my world began.

Seventeen years and ten months ago, it was only when I stepped out of the taxi that I saw the facade of the hotel. A tall tower of iron and glass, with huge picture windows looking out on the city and the ocean, in the distance.

"We're not going to your place?"

"They're doing construction work. I'll explain. I figured you'd be more comfortable here."

"You?"

"Sorry?"

"That *I* would be more comfortable here? Aren't you staying with me?"

The incongruousness of those words. They're etched in my memory. I couldn't get over it. And he was shifting from one foot to the other like a kid who's been caught misbehaving. He cleared his throat. He said we should go and eat something. I must be dead tired. I'd had three meals on board the plane—I didn't need anything, thanks.

I have to speak to you.

I couldn't follow all his explaining. Or, rather, I was trying to understand, but my brain had jet lag. I was reaching for his words, clinging to the last thing he said, as if I were crawling along the roofs of a series of train cars, trying to reach the locomotive. He was talking about some woman, older than we were, more self-assured, too, with a charisma he could not resist. He'd left his apartment to move in with her, it had been so sudden, he didn't expect me to understand, and then it made him very unhappy to hurt me, I meant so much to him.

"Wait."

I pressed the alarm button. The train of his words ground to a halt in his throat.

"Why didn't you tell me all this earlier? When I was still in France? Before I got rid of everything to come here?"

"What do you mean, you got rid of everything?"

"Don't worry about that. Just answer my question."

I remember I was surprised at my own reaction. I didn't go to pieces. I didn't shed a single tear—not just then, not in that place, I'd had my fill of humiliation. I was calm and scathing, but my weapons were useless, the armor he'd made for himself was too thick. He sighed. He murmured that he'd thought that maybe, on seeing me at the airport, his attachment to me would come back like a shot.

"A spark. That's it. I thought there'd be a spark when I saw you again."

"And?"

I didn't need his answer. He didn't give one.

A spark, bastard? A fucking spark? After a fifteen-hour flight? A sleepless night. No shower in two days. The breath of a jackal. A spark? Asshole. Bastard. I still dream of flinging those words in his face. So he'll cower. So I'll strike him. So he'll capitulate, in the end. Because he's weak. Fearful. A coward. No balls. No one can imagine how deeply this affected me. A series of uppercuts.

I rushed out into the blinding Australian daylight. I walked aimlessly through the streets, thinking he was going to follow me, catch up with me, accept the pain, the screams, shit, I deserved at least that. But not at all. At one point I went past the restaurant again and he'd vanished. He'd delivered his message and flown away. Impossible to reach him by phone.

I found a hotel. For two nights. I lay on the bed in that impersonal room, envisaging the various possibilities—in fact, there weren't many. I didn't have enough money to try to start a life here without him. Above all, I didn't have the appropriate visa. There was only one option—back to square one. This square one where I ran into him again, seventeen years later. Incredible.

"We'll go for a drink some other day."

That was it. It came out just like that, a little while ago. Brutally. Right after I raised my head and stared at him. His face was going to pieces. He gave a sort of shudder, a hiccup that went through his entire body. I didn't wait to find out what happened after that. Miraculously, my legs had recovered their agility and energy. In scarcely more than thirty seconds I was out of sight and out of reach.

I wandered around for more than an hour and a half. I went all the way around the city, through the outlying neighborhoods, my steps led me very far, and near the lycée I once attended years ago, there was The Atlantic. Why do I even remember the name, or the proprietor, a peroxide blond with a smoker's voice, who had her favorites and virtually ignored everyone else—I belonged to the second group, of course. Then I went farther still, toward the very edge of town, and of my life, and of his, and of chance and necessity. I didn't manage to calm down. I walked back toward the center. And came upon this café. Le Tom's. I think I must have come here once or twice before I went to Australia. Back then it was called the Dionysus, or the Bacchus. It was so long ago.

I'm alone on the terrace. The rain has driven all the other customers away. The rain is right. Everything needs cleansing. Humiliation. Shame. Words. It's the only way to smother the embers and snuff out the sparks.

9:00 P.M.

JOCELYNE—ON THE TERRACE

I CAME BACK, like I said I would. The café is almost deserted—the customers have left for supper. Ever since they eased up on the restrictions, all the night owls have gotten back into the usual swing of things. They fill the squares in town with their laughter until late at night. Summer has found its bearings. Some people still hesitate—mask or no mask? Kiss on the cheek, or nudge of the elbow, or foot, the way we've learned to do? But their hesitancy is starting to vanish. Until when? The next wave? Or the next speech from the health minister, where he'll impose another turn of the screw? Or the next virus, which will find its way from the wilds of Siberia to come and decimate the planet. I give a shrug—I won't be here anymore to see it. I have no intention of living to a hundred. I've played my role here on earth. I don't wish for such a disease, but if it comes, I won't fight.

I found a place to sit, here on this terrace I struggled so hard to get, and which I had so little opportunity to enjoy when I was the owner of this place. I ordered a Martini Bianco, while waiting for Chloé to join me. Or for Fabrice to come and keep me company. I already know I'll order another one. Tonight I have no limits.

It's strange, this empty terrace—it's like a mini end-of-the-world. I like it best when there's a lot of coming and going, people shouting, back talk and opinions coming from all sides. I often lose myself in other people's conversations. That was both my strength and my weakness when I ran The Atlantic. I felt close to the students who packed the place. I found them awkward and endearing. I played the role of big sister. I poked my nose into things that were none of my business. I melted into their sweet lives—until Michel came along.

There, I've said his name. I've let the dogs loose. I take a quick sip of Martini. Michel is a name that belongs, like this aperitif, to a bygone era. When bars were smoky and I sometimes had to open the windows wide to air the place out, it stank that bad. The ashtrays were overflowing with cigarette butts. Everyone was talking about the rise of the Left. It was a heady time. Michel had come up to me at the central market—he was handing out tracts for the Socialist Party, and I listened to him rattle off his pitch and then countered that as the owner of a bar and fundamentally a capitalist in my soul, I could not, in all decency, take his flyer.

"A bar? Which one?"

It turned out he'd already been to The Atlantic a few times with one of his colleagues. I said goodbye and gave a smile, but he caught up with me a few yards farther along. The local branch was looking for a place to meet, not too far from the center of town, where they could get together for a drink: Would I agree to reserve the room for them one evening a week? They'd pay for their drinks, obviously, and then clean everything up before they left.

The Atlantic closed at eight. I had tried for a while to stay open until late at night, but the place was too far from the actual center. The night owls were drawn to more central places where they could tipple to their hearts' content—like Le Tricasse, Le Montabert, or Le Tom's, which was not yet called Le Tom's, of course, since I was the one who gave it that name.

I agreed to his proposal. They came. All men. I hid behind the bar. Every Wednesday evening, that autumn and winter, I got the feeling I was playing a supporting role in a Claude Sautet movie.

I listened to their diatribes, their arguments, their confrontations. I paid attention. I noticed with some surprise that, in fact, I agreed with quite a few of their proposals— abolition of the death penalty, workers' rights, even if the idea of renationalizing companies scared me and I couldn't shake off the fear that Russian tanks would soon be rolling into Paris. Michel regularly left the table to come and get their orders, and make sure I wasn't bored, and to ask me how he and his comrades could thank me. I simply replied that they could send me their kids, to boost my turnover. One day he asked me what I thought about all their palaver. I replied that it was enriching, to listen to their sparring matches. I confessed that, on social issues, I often shared their opinions. He nodded. And so I added, "But still . . ." And a smile lit up his face. He had a genuine smile, Michel did. Broad. Radiant. A smile that made you trust him.

"But still—what?"

"Is that it, you're all there? What I mean is, are all the members of the local branch here tonight?"

"Yes, except Jacques, because he's working in Paris. Why?"

"Nothing strikes you as odd?"

He took a step back. He listened to his friends clashing swords. He frowned. No, really, he couldn't see.

"Half of humanity is missing, Michel."

"Pardon?"

"Women. I suppose you only see them as secretaries or hairdressers or bookkeepers. Journalists, if pressed, but for fashion magazines."

"Not at all! We have great respect for the women in the other camp. Simone Veil, for example!"

"I don't see any Simone Veils in here. Just a bunch of guys drinking and claiming they're changing the world. In other words, your typical bistro crowd. I hope your offspring will help things evolve. For you lot, it's too late. You're too content just to go home to your tidy house, with the kids in bed and tomorrow's lunch waiting in Tupperware. What's more, I'm sure that most of your wives work, it's important, right, equality between the sexes, and their salary most of all, but—"

"I'm not married, Jocelyne. I don't live with anyone. I'm a real old bachelor."

"You're not old."

"I'm thirty-eight, actually. Ten years older than you, no? And anyway, you're absolutely right. How can we get more women into politics?"

"By imposing parity."

"What?"

"One woman, one man—on every ticket. Require at least fifty percent women in parliament. Just one example among others."

He stood there motionless for a few seconds. His eyes narrowed. He continued to smile. He wasn't strikingly handsome. It was something else—almost ethereal. Then he let out a sort of long whistle, and tilted his head to one side.

"Well, you really are a radical!"

"Liberty, equality, fraternity. Haven't you noticed? Women don't always have the liberty to do what they want, they don't have access to equality, and they're outright excluded from the word 'fraternity'— that's for brothers, a guy thing, people with balls, in other words. Believe me. It's only in capitalist countries that women will win the fight. There's never been a woman head of state in the USSR."

"Or in the USA."

"Or in France. The only example that springs to mind, I'm sorry to say, is Thatcher."

His face creased into a grimace of disgust. I went on.

"Yes, it hurts, doesn't it? You should get back to your friends. They're getting impatient and they have urgent, important business to attend to. And anyway, you're going to have to strike camp before long because both you and I have to go to work tomorrow."

"You run this place on your own?"

"And I'm proud of it."

"You're never afraid?"

"Of what? A few winos? Inveterate womanizers?"

"Jocelyne, can I . . . No, it's ridiculous."

"If you want to ask me if you can take me out for a drink somewhere else, yes, that's a stupid idea. I don't give my business to the competition. Especially not the bars run by the Lebrun brothers. Hooligans of the worst kind."

He stood there, hesitant, and I patted him on his right shoulder, an almost maternal gesture.

"On the other hand, if you'd like to invite me to your place . . . "

I saw the gleam of panic in his eyes, and I could imagine the untidy apartment, the dirty sheets, the vacuum cleaner standing in a corner, the unemptied ashtrays, and the window never opened. I didn't think there would be any other female presence, patiently awaiting the hero's return. I trusted him, what he'd told me. A lone wolf. I don't really know how you resist them, those guys.

" . . . or if you'd like some herbal tea, at my place."

That's it. That's how one thing led to another. Michel and I didn't leave together, so that the others wouldn't suspect anything; we didn't want any off-color remarks or bawdy jokes—I heard them all day long. I drew the curtains, closed the door, and made as if I was going home. He joined me at the top of Rue Édouard-Vaillant.

I neglected my lycée students. And anyway, I existed only at the edge of their existence. It was time for me to build my own. Or let's just say that it was time for me to make a detour from the path I'd been going down. I was declaring my independence. I'd joined the women's movement, but I voted conservative—I wasn't keeping track of every petty contradiction. I'd been taking the pill, and then I followed my doctor's advice: he told me to be careful, because pill plus smoking meant cancer for sure in the next ten years. It was all very messy. And then I got pregnant. From one day to the next, not another drop of alcohol.

I take a sip of my Martini. I'll make sure I can cope this time. I'll follow my story through to the end. The sun is setting on summer 2021. All over town you can hear people shouting as they stride along the pedestrian streets, they want the inhabitants to know they're alive and they don't give a fuck. They'll disappear soon, too, they'll be lured to the new neighborhoods on the edge of town, where there's the multiplex with its cluster of chain restaurants, and the bowling alley, with its delightfully retro atmosphere, and the parks, farther out.

Thomas.

That's the name I gave him, but it's private. It was never registered anywhere. He really existed, and he never really existed. Life is like that, sometimes.

I got pregnant when Michel and I had been lovers for six months—yes, I know, it makes you smile, those old-fashioned expressions like "lovers," "mistresses," "liaisons," but what we had between us meant more than just sleeping together. That's what I liked to believe, anyway, and I'm still convinced of it. A free, happy union. I'm sure that he saw us as a couple like Sartre and de Beauvoir, even though we had very little in common with them, my political opinions for a start, which were rooted in notions of individualism and private property. I didn't have any idols or historical models, for myself. I lived in the present moment. That was probably the one and only time in my life when I didn't try to control what happened, but was simply happy to enjoy. He would come to my place after work, or meet me at the café. Some people even thought at one point that I'd hired a waiter.

He worked for the national railroad. He was trying, with others, to rescue the network of freight trains, which was struggling. Trucks were taking over, everywhere, going through villages, polluting for all they were worth, causing accidents, but no one found fault with them—door-to-door transport was ever so much more practical. He was a militant, and he believed with all his might that a change in government could reverse the tendency. I was torn between laughter and pity.

He wasn't married and didn't want to be. His parents' relationship had been tumultuous—which, in those days, meant the husband abused his wife and called her every name in the book, not hesitating to humiliate her in front of guests. They eventually got divorced when Michel was still an adolescent. He was relieved but he swore never to make the same mistake. Every human being must be free to choose their own destiny. I made fun of him, pointing out that this faith in personal success and hatred of community was hardly in keeping with a socialist-communist outlook. We got along well. We could have been a fine couple.

He was a good man, Michel. He didn't want to be a father, but he said all the right things, from "I'll be there, whatever you decide," to "There are no problems, only solutions." I hesitated—the time frame was very tight. In the end I decided to keep the baby. Michel opened a bottle of champagne. I made him promise not to tell anyone for as long as we could keep it hidden. I could imagine some people might look puzzled, trying to blend our features; we really didn't look right together. Everyone was sure that Michel would rise through the ranks at the railways and become a manager, particularly as he'd have the political wind in his sails, since he'd been a militant right from the beginning. I was amused by his new show of timidity—he no longer dared penetrate me, he was afraid of bumping, hitting, causing bleeding. He'd been reading up. He'd heard of placenta previa. I rolled my eyes and continued to work as busily as ever at the café, to go on with life as I pleased, along with a slight reduction in the number of cigarettes, not a drop of alcohol, and a regular urge to rush to the toilet. For a while, life was sparkling.

And then, one day, life lost its sparkle.

I don't want to go into the details. For years I'd been prey to nightmares—at night or during the day. Sometimes they'd come for me in the middle of an ordinary day while I was serving a customer, I'd turn around and then, all of a sudden, there'd be this dark space before me, with a bleeding embryo emerging from it. Honestly, I don't know how I survived at times. Especially when stomach cramps occurred at the same time. I would tell people I'd eaten something that didn't agree with me.

It never agreed with me. You can well imagine.

In the sixth month, I woke up, terrified. I couldn't feel anything anymore. Michel had already left for work. I spoke to my belly. No. That's the limit. I don't want to go back into all that. My words. My pleading. By that point they were no use. I went straight to the E.R. The woman at the reception had a sour expression but when I explained what was going on her behavior suddenly changed. I became a priority—she'd been there herself, she assured me that impressions could often be misleading—take her daughter, who was healthy and strong; she'd find me an OB/GYN right away.

There was no miracle. Only pain. They told me the fetus was a boy, but they didn't ask me if I wanted to see him. In those days, they hid things. They thought it was better that way. And anyway, I would have said no, point-blank. It was out of the question for me to mourn, to try to find closure, as they say nowadays. They had to keep me in the hospital because there were complications, in addition to all the rest—at one point I'd heard a nurse say, her voice faltering, "We're losing her," and I knew they weren't talking about the child. I was about to go with him. They saved me. In return, reproduction would become a complicated matter. No need to spell it out. I would remain a non-mother.

I got rid of everything. I closed The Atlantic. I couldn't bear the prospect of being forced to listen to sob stories about broken hearts, or the enthusiastic outbursts of other people's children. I didn't want to take on Michel's sorrow, either. That was unfair, I know, but I was giving myself that right. To this day I still believe that men suffer less than women do, in such circumstances. For a start, their flesh hasn't been ravaged, and flesh is what we are, and what we'll remain, deep down: bones and skin. I crossed Michel off the list of my contacts—along with all my local friends and acquaintances.

I thought about the people I loved or had loved. About the ones who'd touched me, or moved me. Those I could still help, maybe. There were nights when the constant stream of thoughts would not stop. One day I got back on my feet. I still don't know why. I took my car and drove for hours to the Atlantic coast. The ocean was wild.

I rented a house by the beach for two months. The resort was deserted. The real estate agent informed me that for anything like shopping or services, such as doctors or the post office, I'd have to go to the town six miles from there. I nodded. He hesitated for a moment then he added that it was rare for people to rent off-season, to be sure, but it did happen. People getting over the end of an affair. Digesting the news of a sickness. A death to mourn. A novel to write. I let him go on—I figured he wanted to reassure me, bring me into a sort of community of pain, where we could all belong, and from which we would emerge, after a few weeks, strengthened and heartened, full of vigor to confront the reckless race of existence, the one that leads straight to the grave. He handed me the keys to a little house with blue shutters, located on Rue des Comètes.

That first week I did nothing but sleep. The second week the same. Then I was surrounded by a comatose grayness that wasn't just a reflection of the ocean weather. Conscientiously choosing the time they would be the most empty, I took the car and went around the shops. I bought some notebooks that had big pages of graph paper with squares. I did some bookkeeping. I toyed for a day or two with the possibility of becoming one of those vagabond types who were no longer in fashion, but some of whom still wandered the earth with their backpack and their thirst for contact with the local population, who found them amusing and annoying by turns. But I wasn't made of such stuff. I've sometimes regretted it. I would have liked to possess José's urge to dive headlong into adventure. I thought about changing professions as well—but I had hardly any experience in any other field, and there weren't many that tempted me. I was probably born to be a café owner. Alone, holding my own against the drunken customers, flying the smart-ass-attitude flag—fearless and above reproach. A hard-headed woman, as they say. Flamboyant.

After a month and a half I'd had enough of the ocean—all its color had returned, and it glistened with sunlight. I knew I'd be back, in any case. This was where Thomas was, for me. This was where I'd buried him, mentally. We'd decided to call him Thomas, if it was a boy. Cécile, if it was a girl. Like all parents, we'd spent hours hesitating over the names, writing up lists where we crossed some off as the days went by. Very late one night, only Thomas and Cécile were left. Michel and I looked at each other. Thomas or Cécile. Decided. Michel had laughed—the only references that came to mind, for him, were religious. Sainte Cécile, patron saint of musicians. And Saint Thomas the Incredulous, who believed only what he could see.

I believe only what I can see.

I didn't see him.

No. Pointless feeling sorry for myself. I'm an old woman. I stand up to life. Now as in the past.

Life went on. When Michel came through the door of The Atlantic I was very clear. No going back. He didn't insist. Drab years went by. The adolescents put some color back into my everyday life. I lost myself in their stories, once again. After playing the role of big sister, I became a maternal figure. And then, bit by bit, the café lost its appeal. They looked for other places to go. Far away from the lycée. Far away from the neighborhood. They relocated. The decline was as rapid as it had been sudden.

I sold The Atlantic. I was lucky—and I needed some luck. The owners of the bank next door wanted to expand. They offered me a very good price—double what I thought I'd get. I also sold the plot of land my grandmother had made me swear to pass on to my heirs no matter what. That was convenient: I wouldn't be having any heirs.

I'd known Franck Palancher for over thirty years. He was one of my mother's neighbors. He still frequently called me "the kid," even though I was almost sixty. When I found out he was going to close down, I stood right in front of him and said I was prepared to take over his business. He nearly dropped the cigarette that was always hanging from the corner of his mouth. He took me to one side in what was still the storage room, where Chloé now settles down every morning. He was deadly serious—I'd never seen him like that, this man who had a reputation as a rather jovial guy. It took me a few minutes to realize that he was telling me off—trying to dissuade me. Of course he knew I had experience in running cafés, but whoa, this wouldn't be the same sort of clientele, at all—no more gangs of penniless but respectful kids who'd end up telling you their entire life story. This would be something else altogether: tough. You'll get people who order a little glass of dry white wine or a beer at seven in the morning and they'll keep knocking them back, as many as eight, before they go to clock in to work, not before they let off steam kicking a few homeless folk and calling them good-for-nothings. You'll get men who wolf whistle whenever a girl comes in, and she'll have to beat a hasty retreat or else stand up to them. Then you've got the petty crooks who set up meetings for their trafficking—things they claim fell off the truck, pathetic deals, but as a result from time to time you'll get a visit from the law. And then there's all the cigarette smoke, and the Lotto players who try to prove to you by A + B that they've won and they scream at the machine when it refuses to give them what they think they're owed, even though they just don't know how to read the numbers, or they just really want to believe they've won. You need patience. Strength. An iron hand. Though you could hire Tony, he's used to it.

Tony.

In fact, his name was Antoine. With the years he'd spent at the gym, he'd given himself the build of an athlete. No one went picking fights with Tony. No one knew that his passion was photographing birds. People pictured him on Sunday taking his motorbike and meeting up with buddies like himself, but in fact he'd climb into his Twingo and head straight for the forests where you could still walk around without getting a volley of lead in your ass, and with his camera on its strap, he'd spend hours bird-watching, ready to press the shutter. He talked about his sparrows. I hired him on the spot.

The clientele of the place changed very gradually. A woman running a bar, it makes waves. The small-time dealers don't really like the idea—when they glanced at me, they immediately thought of their mother or their sisters. They changed their watering hole. Others started coming—acquaintances, tourists—people Franck had never managed to attract. One summer, Tony wanted to redecorate with some of his pals. It wasn't altogether to my taste, but it was definitely better than before. We'd become bougie. And then Tony fell in love with the vice president of the League for the Protection of Birds. He was over forty. She taught life and earth sciences. She'd asked for a transfer so she could be nearer her aging parents. She got it. They lived apart for a year, meeting up only for those few days of vacation they had in common. I was the one who urged Tony to make the move. I assured him that the café would get on fine without him, now that we'd changed its public image. I also promised him I'd go and visit them in Vendôme from time to time. I was careful not to, in fact. They had better things to do. He wrote to announce the birth of their first child, a boy, and then the second one, a girl.

I lasted three more years, then one evening, as I was closing, I felt the entire weight of everything I'd been through on my shoulders—it's strange, don't you think? One minute you're full of energy and making plans, then the next, you sit on the stool, shake your head, and think, *That's it, it's over.*

I'd accumulated enough money to keep my house here and treat myself to a little apartment on the Atlantic coast. I would pretend to believe that Thomas couldn't come and see me because he was sailing the seven seas and going to meet other people, with an open face and laughing eyes. One foot in my fictional invention, the other one here, in this reality I've known all my life—watching the slow evolution of this café that will never replace The Atlantic in my heart, but which I'm glad to see is still standing, despite the global disasters of these last two years. What I'm proudest of is having found the ideal successor. A kind, discreet person. Loyal. Someone I've watched grow up all these years. Who would say hello to me whenever I ran into him and exchange a few words with me, just like that, for no reason, in memory of the afternoons he'd spent at The Atlantic, telling me about his disappointments in love. Who was trying to find his place in the town and couldn't. I'm lucky, in the end. I have two sons. One who's going all around the world, real or imaginary, and another, who isn't mine but who will carry on my work. Not everyone is that fortunate.

I can feel Fabrice's hand squeezing mine. They both came over, awhile ago, José and him, and they've been sitting in silence at my table. It's to them I've been telling my story. They haven't moved an inch. They're my watchdogs. Standing guard. Suddenly, Fabrice is fidgeting next to me. *Oh, hey, look who's coming! Over here, Chloé, I was just babbling. Nothing interesting. Old women's stuff. But let's not stay outside. The wind's picked up and there are nasty gusts. Let's go inside, and you guys buy me a round, for God's sake! We have so many things to celebrate. No, José, you're not going home. You have to stay. You're an integral part of the story now. Shall we sit at the table in the back, Chloé? It's been waiting for you since this morning. It can't do without you anymore.*

CHLOÉ

"I WARN YOU, I'm not very comfortable with the notion of a family council. Or with the concept of the family, period. All those people saying over and over all day long that friends are the family we choose, it makes me sick."

It's true, after all. There they are, all three of them, sitting there, the mother and her two pseudosons. As if they were in one of those imposing paintings from the nineteenth century that have pride of place in the Musée d'Orsay. I hesitated for a long time before coming back to Le Tom's this evening. Reemerging from the cocoon I've been in these last eighteen months. But I promised Jocelyne—and I wanted to see Fabrice at night. It's been such a long time since I aroused even a hint of desire, since I felt the slightest thing in the company of a man, so I was curious to see how things might evolve.

Opposite us, they're not very responsive. José has put on some quiet background music, I think it's Suzanne Vega, an American singer my mother used to listen to when I was little, but I wouldn't stake my life on it. Jocelyne is the first to speak and her husky voice echoes in the empty room.

"We're not friends, as far as I know."

I can't help but smile and raise my left thumb.

"What's more," she continues, pointing at José, "if this guy here were my son, he'd be about to become a prodigal one. José is going to leave us to go wandering around the world. First stop?"

"Scotland."

"A cold place where it rains—when it's not snowing—and you can walk for hours without seeing a living soul. True or false?"

"Technically, it's possible. But I'm going to settle in the Southern Highlands. Not far from Loch Ness. I have friends who're renovating a farm."

"But hey, nothing grows in Scotland, except beer!"

"We'll check that out, when you come to see me there, Jocelyne. It'll make a change from your seaside resorts where all you do is stare at the horizon and wait for death."

"I like Scotland."

They all turn and look at me.

"Well, what I mean is that I went there once and I have good memories. But that's probably because I'm a girl who likes the cold."

"And you, Fabrice, how would you define yourself?"

A dubious expression and a murmur: "Temperate, I suppose." I refrain from saying that now that's exactly what I'm looking for. Temperate. The seasons we used to have when I was little, even though my mother maintains that everything was already out of whack long before. Showers. Patches of blue. Fleecy clouds. In a landscape like that, yes, I could find my place.

"When, exactly, did you get back here, Chloé?"

I open my eyes a little wider: that's the first time José has ever spoken to me without sounding aggressive, and his voice is deep, and gentle.

"Just before the first lockdown. Out in public, in Vantaa, everyone was talking about the same thing. Wuhan. And Italy, above all. Travelers who came back from Lombardy had caught the virus and gone into quarantine. They were starting to consider exceptional emergency measures, both economic and medical. We were afraid there'd be a global economic crash. That all the schools, public places, borders, would be closed. The same thing as here, wasn't it? I heard people talking about all that—but I was elsewhere. In some inner wandering. I was behaving like a robot at the tearoom, and sometimes it shocked the customers. There were fewer and fewer of them, in any case. People were beginning to shelter in place, at home."

Initially, I had imagined going around the world—a new uprooting, temporary jobs and, above all, no emotional attachments. A bit like José, now. But from one day to the next the planet seemed to have ganged up on me. Videos of Chinese in their tower blocks were shown on social media, and the Italians were about to come next, and then the rest of the world, no doubt, now that viruses went global; no one could stop the progression of the disease and it turned into an epidemic, then a pandemic. It was easy to see where it was all leading—being stuck for weeks on end in out-of-the-way places; being feared and rejected if you caught the disease; storefront shutters pulled down, doors double locked. Only a few countries would avoid the full range of security measures, but we knew from the start that there'd be even less reason to trust their governments, because they were ruled by cranks who denied the proof there in front of them, shouting that it was all "fake news," or calling for capsules or herbal teas that would clean out your organism from head to toe.

I had a few sleepless nights—but that didn't change much since my sleep had been irregular for nearly six months already—and then I finally resigned myself to calling my mother. I could sense her reluctance when I mentioned coming back, but I immediately reassured her that I had no intention of interfering with the happiness she'd finally rediscovered with her new partner, or of coming and bothering her in the south. I just wanted to move back into the place that had been my home long ago—for the time it would take to see where this grotesque health crisis was taking us; the time, too, for me to get myself sorted out and understand what kind of life I wanted to live. My mother's voice, relieved, reedy, on the line—she understood very well, she herself had only just found out, late in life, that she could be fulfilled in her relationship (and sexually, too, she insisted, while I winced as if I'd just bitten into a lemon). "'Those who never try are only mistaken once,' said I don't remember which philosopher," she added, learnedly. I refrained from pointing out that she was actually quoting the singer-songwriter

Véronique Sanson. My unexpected arrival actually suited her. She was afraid that with the panic caused by the pandemic strangers might become squatters in vacant houses. This way at least people would know the house was inhabited. The neighbors would just have to be notified.

It was only once I'd hung up that I noticed she never asked me at any point why I was coming back.

(I can feel their eyes on me—it could almost make me blush. It's been so long since I was the center of attention. Because in my threesome with Annika and Ari it wasn't me. And I couldn't exactly say who it was, among us, who drew people's gazes. Annika, perhaps. She was so radiant. I make a mental correction: She "is" so radiant. There's no reason why her joie de vivre should have vanished. On the contrary, surely. It's just that she has become one of those sepia images that inhabit my memory, fading, bit by bit. I had lots of photographs of Annika, Ari, and myself, then last year, when I was sitting out on the porch in the silence of an April night, I erased everything. Conscientiously. Meticulously. Every trace. Of the others. Then of myself. I deleted all my social media accounts. I methodically searched for references where my name or my career came up and tried to wipe them away. This is an inhuman, almost pointless task nowadays. I succeeded only very partially. If you really look, you can find me. In the archives of a local Finnish newspaper. On pictures taken at the tearoom.)

I'm not sure I can pinpoint when, exactly, we became a three-headed entity.

What I do recall, perfectly, however, is the moment when I found the two of them naked, in the bed in the apartment next to the tearoom, where, normally, Annika met the pregnant couples she was seeing. Paradoxically, I was the one who was most embarrassed, and it was at that moment more than any other that I became most aware of our cultural differences—the two of them with their uninhibited nudity and a certain degree of embarrassment, to be sure, but not that much guilt, in the end. Then me, with the upbringing my parents had given me—this tendency to believe that you were doomed to fail. That life was a violent storm and that the aim, above all, was to try to find shelter, or dodge the rain. And then there was my relation with my body. This body my mother had rarely spoken to me about—my period, dispatched in five minutes, sexuality seen only from the point of view of reproduction or venereal disease.

I stood there like an idiot, arms dangling, while they were stretching their limbs and trying to make light of the confusion, telling me that in fact, they'd been meaning to have a word with me. But wouldn't I rather just take my clothes off and lie down next to them instead? Annika would give me a massage while Ari caressed my hair.

Someone coughs.

I'm brought brutally back to the room in the café. Across from me Jocelyne, very focused, is hunting for the words that could act as a balm on my wounds. José, next to her, eyes narrowed, a deep wrinkle across his forehead, is wondering what he would have done in my shoes. I'm sure he would have been less of a nitwit. He would probably have tried his luck, like I did, but he would've put his heart into it. He wouldn't have stayed on the edge of the pool, his feet dangling in the water—whereas that was the impression I must have given; I realize that now.

And then there's Fabrice. He was the one who choked on the sip of gin he tried to take, to make the pill go down. He excuses himself. No one notices. I continue the story. The expression, "drain one's cup to the last drop" goes through my mind, but there was no cup, nor was there any last drop. It was much less dramatic and also much more complicated than that.

I joined them and we became a ménage à trois. There were often five of us living there, actually, because Annika's children were with us half the time. We almost never brought up the situation, Annika and I. It was not for a lack of trying, on her part. She thought we should express what we felt in order to bring to light our inhibitions and our joys, our frustration and euphoria. She'd already had a relationship of this nature as an adolescent, and to her it felt delicious to be immersed in something similar again. That was her very word, she insisted, because Ari and I were delicious, like the cakes I made for the tearoom.

Six months.

Half a year spent running with the hare and hunting with the hounds. That first time, the weather was still warm, but you could feel how summer was about to pack up and leave. Ari seemed to look at me differently. He confided one day that he'd thought I'd be incapable of engaging in such an experience, and he'd been astonished by my reaction, even if he still found me somewhat reserved.

"But that's your nature," he added. "Deep down, it's the way you are. You're a spectator who plays along with the world from time to time but is often on the edge. I'm sure you'd make an excellent painter or artist—you have a gift for observation. With this innocent expression on your face, you glance at your customers, you say a few words to them, and they tell you their story. It's a pity, on the other hand, that you never share your own story."

"It's because I don't have one, Ari. My life is uneventful."

"I don't believe a word of it. And if, alas, that has been the case, then your life is turning eventful now, with us."

With us. I picked up on that, yes. Ari often used the word "we" or "us" when he meant himself and Annika. He didn't realize. He was reestablishing that comfortable border between two natives and the foreign tourist, without ever remembering that the "we," until not so long ago, meant him and me. Of course it bothered me, but I can't say that I didn't get anything out of it. I discovered zones of pleasure I didn't even know existed. The blush on Ari's neck when Annika and I embraced. The respect I earned in his eyes.

I noticed fairly soon that in fact, if all this hadn't happened, Ari and I would have split up before much longer. We hardly touched each other anymore. There had been passion, in the beginning, but then, quite soon, we began to have sex less and less often. I think I didn't give him enough of an opportunity to shine. In this country where equality between men and women has been raised to the status of dogma, Ari needed to see a glow in the eyes of his conquests, a glow of unbridled admiration. Admiration for his enterprising spirit. For the brilliance of some of his ideas. For his physique, which he maintained with long jogs in nature—but I realize I'm being silly, there was probably less jogging and more lovemaking than I thought. For that ability he had to fix things from floor to ceiling, and lose himself in carpentry or plumbing, showing the same aptitude as for finance or computer science. Ari's father kept telling me that I'd been very lucky to meet his son, and I must deploy all my charms to keep him; then Ari's mother would give him a pat on the arm or the shoulder and take me to one side—she was not convinced there was actually a great good fortune of which I would be the beneficiary. She'd been observing her son for years and there was a side of him she could not fathom. A hardness. A darkness. Anyway. Which did not mean, she added, that we did not make a lovely couple. She loved the idea of cross-cultural exchange. I smiled. I wasn't sure that was what she really felt.

During those few months of weightlessness, I had ample opportunity to study the dark side of the man I'd thought I would marry. As did Annika, actually. From almost one minute to the next he could become very distant, and we never knew exactly where we stood. As for Annika, she was easier to read. And frank. If there is one person I miss from Vantaa, it's her. Our fits of laughter. Our raptures, as well. The way we had, too, of ganging up sometimes against the male, who denied he was dominating but didn't hesitate to give orders.

All three of us knew it wouldn't last, and it was this awareness of the precariousness of the situation that gave such flamboyance to our relationship—in the eyes of others, in any case. Because we didn't hide from anything—except Annika's and Ari's families, of course—although I'm quite sure they would have taken it well. After all, we were in those final years when we could "experiment with life" before transitioning into the strange time of our thirties, when we'd have to try to forget that every day we go through the same motions and the verb "have" gradually mutates into what we swore it would never become: a purpose. An obsession, even.

It was a kind of sleepwalking. In the morning Ari woke up early to go running, whatever the temperature. I got up shortly after, had a quick breakfast, and went to the tearoom. I immersed myself in all the prep work—patisserie requires organization more than anything. I compiled the recipes and varied the menus, invariably adding the lemon meringue pie my mother systematically refused to buy for me when I was little, because "it's a rich pie for rich people, let them poison themselves with it," and the fondant au chocolat-crème anglaise, which I knew Annika could not resist. I didn't make cakes for Ari. Ari didn't have a sweet tooth. Ari could be biting, period.

Annika would stop by during the morning, between two appointments. She held some of them at the apartment next to the tearoom, which Ari and his friends had painstakingly soundproofed. Other couples preferred to have their sessions in their own home. She listened to them talk about their fears, reassured them, helped them to picture life with a child. She even spoke openly about her status as a single mom, the plus sides she enjoyed and the disadvantages she'd confronted. Oddly enough, this reassured them: So, life does go on. The baby wasn't necessarily going to mean the end of their youth, even if that was what, deep down, they both wanted. Annika would massage the mother's belly as well, and talk to the child-to-be. She showed them how they could communicate with the baby—how it moved around, following the placement of their hands.

That was it. We stayed in that bubble for nearly six months. And then one evening, not long after the Christmas holidays, when we were about to start watching one of those must-see TV series, Annika suddenly felt very tired and asked us to excuse her. She'd had a stressful day. She was going home, unusually. She needed to have some time alone.

We found ourselves face-to-face, Ari and I—and we gradually became aware of the abyss that had come between us. A real Grand Canyon we were flying over in a silent helicopter while we put away what was left over from the meal, which we'd hardly touched, while exchanging a few onomatopoeias. We lasted for two hours and then Ari asked me—always very polite, Ari was—if I would mind if he went out for a beer with some colleagues from work. He'd turned them down more than once and he was afraid that they'd stop inviting him. He joked and said that my ears and Annika's would certainly be burning because all his friends were very intrigued by our so-called "third option," but his joke fell flat on the kitchen tiles. I knew perfectly well that he was going to Annika's place, to try to figure out her sudden volte-face. I smiled—I trusted her. She wouldn't answer the bell. She'd stay locked in the dark. She had even less need for him on his own than of the two of us together. It's true, I remember having thought just that. And then I heard the pinging sound which meant an incoming text message. It was short. It said she'd gone home to take a pregnancy test. Now she was sure she was pregnant and she didn't know what to do. She wanted me to be the first to know. Before Ari. It was a tactful thought. I answered that any decision she made belonged to her alone, that it wasn't triple, or double—and whatever her decision, she would realize, sooner or later, it was the right one. I was drowning my dismay in empty talk. Another message. The problem, Annika added, was that she was in love with the threesome, and not just the father.

I grabbed a jacket in the entrance and went out into the night. I still don't understand why I absolutely wanted to go to the Helsinki Data and Demographic Services— a three-hour walk from there. Maybe because, in this country, that's where turning points in life are recorded—marriages, divorces, declarations of parenthood. I went through the Kinapori neighborhood. There weren't many people out on the streets. Finns had been staying home over recent weeks. I hurried straight ahead, like a robot. At one point I found myself outside a travel agency, on the ground floor of a tall building. I stared for a long time in the window, then a woman came to open the door with a smile. She confirmed that, because it was late, everything was closed, but she said that if there was anything—a brochure or a destination—I was interested in, she could make an exception and give me the information. I mumbled my thanks. I murmured that I was a bit lost. I didn't even notice that I wasn't speaking English but had turned to my mother tongue.

"Are you French?"

I nodded.

"Do you want to go home?"

I burst into tears and I was as astonished as anyone. The woman across from me—Katarina, she told me—was so disconcerted that she offered me a coffee. She'd expected anything but this. She'd stayed late at the office because she had tasks to finish and no one was expecting her at home this evening, but to have a Frenchwoman show up at almost ten p.m., on the verge of imploding, was the last thing she could have imagined. She went on talking while she made the coffee, still smiling. Women who run travel agencies are well-acquainted with surprises in life, and are masters of the unexpected— emergency surgeries and cancer diagnoses putting all the family's plans on hold, vacation paradises turning into nightmares because of a tsunami. She took the opportunity to give me a few brochures about weekends in Paris, on the Atlantic or Mediterranean coasts, and in Brittany, too: Apparently for several years now her clients seemed more and more drawn to that region, had I been there? I smiled. I said that I'd been there on vacation once, yes, with my parents when I was little, but that I had no real memories. The only images that remained were those which had pride of place in family albums: a little girl in a red tracksuit and a yellow cotton sun hat, opening her eyes wide at the sight of the sea; the same little girl on a merry-go-round, riding a wooden horse called Pegasus. But, I muttered, I didn't want to trouble her with my stories, she must think I was crazy and I'd already imposed on her kindness long enough.

"People who weep aren't crazy. It's the ones who don't shed a tear who end up with a rope around their neck or drowned in the harbor. Come back and see me when you've decided. But, in fact, you already have, haven't you?"

It was when I murmured, "Yes," that I realized how far I had come in just a few hours. It was the end of February. I wanted to go home. Before closing the door, Katarina told me that, at any other time, she probably would have advised me to give it some thought, weigh the pros and cons, but things were different now. The international situation was worrying, she was convinced that the borders were about to close and that travel would be forbidden for a long time to come.

As I'd predicted, Ari didn't come back to the apartment. The following morning I didn't open the tearoom. I stayed in one of the armchairs, thinking and working things out. How much I had in the bank here. What I had saved up back in France. The savings account I'd never touched. How long could I reasonably last without working? At least I'd have no rent to pay. My mother's house was big and empty. There was a garden. I'd have peace and quiet. One way or another I'd get by in France.

So I got out of Finland.

Annika and Ari were far too preoccupied with her pregnancy to notice my moods. Ari was strangely calm, almost absent. A constant smile lingered on his lips—the ancestral satisfaction of the male, proud of procreating, no doubt. As for Annika, she seemed far more preoccupied. She claimed it was because she didn't know how to explain the situation to the couples she was seeing. If the first trimester went smoothly, then it wouldn't be a problem. But if she began to feel nauseous and was constantly tired, as had been the case with her eldest boy, she could no longer be a doula for anyone other than herself. She had long, passionate conversations with her sister doulas. For my part, I was dealing with administrative issues and getting my belongings together. Tidying my room.

In the end I invented an ailment for my mother. I said I'd gotten a distressed phone call from her. Worrying blood tests. There was a strong likelihood that what the doctors had found was cancerous. I embroidered: My mother was alone, and terrified. I didn't really have any choice. I couldn't leave her in such a distraught state, particularly as she went into a panic whenever she heard the news about the Chinese virus and the way it attacked the most vulnerable organisms.

Annika and Ari sympathized. The nodded their heads a lot; they put their arms around me a lot. I had to get back to France, of course, but we'd be in touch every day, in any case. We'd Skype or WhatsApp every evening. I'd show them my childhood home, since they realized they'd never seen any pictures of it. And they, too, would speak to my mother. Annika in particular. Even with the language barrier, she was sure she could find the words, the tone, or the attitude. We hesitated, regarding the lease on the tearoom—but it would probably be best to terminate it. We'd find a way to reopen as soon as I came back. Ari proved to be very considerate. Ari was no fool. He suspected I wouldn't be coming back any time soon.

They went with me to the airport. I hadn't been back there since my arrival. The departure time was somewhat delayed. I told them not to stay, it was too much of a cliché and not like us—and anyway, as soon as my mother felt better or I knew she had good people around her I'd be back, it was a matter of just a month or two at the most, and by then Annika's belly would have grown, or not, but in any case, everything would be fine. No one had died. Only death is final, and tragic, right?

They were taken aback. They'd never heard me go on like this. I was babbling on and on. I'd been transformed into one of those specialists who come out on stage at international conferences and rattle on with great confidence and a touch of irony about very serious topics, such as artificial intelligence or climate change. I kissed them both on the lips. They had tears in their eyes and I was glad I could produce that sort of effect. I walked away, like the heroine of a film, without looking back, waving the fingers of my left hand as I went straight to the departure lounge.

What happened after that, to be honest, is all a blur.

I remember hearing my flight called over the loud-speaker. A guy in a yellow sweater bumped into me then apologized, saying it was really stupid, this tendency we all had to rush to the gate, as if there wasn't going to be enough space for everyone. The same guy ended up sitting across the aisle from me. He told me his name was Yvan, although he wasn't even Breton. He added that he'd sussed out right away that I was French—well, on a flight from Helsinki to Paris the odds were fifty-fifty after all, right? I gave a vague smile. I could have stopped him from continuing, but I liked listening to him—to him, and to the language he was speaking and that I was rediscovering as my own. I felt as if I were moving through a pool of words, tirelessly swimming laps, even though for several years there'd been a constant back-and-forth between Finnish, Swedish, and English with the occasional, but very rare, touch of French.

"Lightning visit or long stay?" he asked.

"Return. Temporary or for good, I don't know yet."

"Anyway, we're all going to be stuck somewhere for months, at the rate the virus is spreading."

"You think so?"

"Haven't you been following the news?"

"I have, but I still can't quite believe it."

"That's normal, it's never happened before. And everyone is watching the show, and can't do a thing. There isn't even a wave of panic. Although it's bound to happen sooner or later. When governments decide to impose restrictions on the population, there'll be a stampede for the supermarkets."

"That's pointless, you can't make your fridge any bigger."

"There are entire basements devoted to freezers, you know. All over the world. And then there are people who've been preparing for medical disasters for years. They're prepared for battle. Armed to the teeth. They're waiting for the apocalypse and they think the coming pandemic is a sign from God. So you see, we're not out of the woods yet."

"What do you do? Are you a journalist?"

"I'm a doctor. Epidemiologist. I can tell they're going to need me at home so I'm going back."

"And why were you in Finland?"

"International program. Cooperation."

"That's good. I wish I had such an exciting life."

"What makes you think it's exciting?"

"At the moment, in any case."

He gave a short laugh. I added that I ran a tearoom in Vantaa, in the suburbs of Helsinki, but that my personal life got a bit complicated recently and I needed some time and distance to think about things. The customary excuse. Apparently I'd have plenty of time now, by the sound of it.

"I don't know what the Finns are going to do. The Swedes seem to be leaning rather toward herd immunity. Letting the virus perform natural selection. It's astonishing, coming from people who pride themselves on being among the most progressive on the planet. You'll have Wi-Fi, where you're going,

I hope? Because we're going to spend the coming months glued to our screens."

I saw him again, often—on those famous screens. He appeared regularly on the 24-hour news channels. He commented on charts and graphics, and didn't hesitate, either, to criticize some of the measures the government was taking—he insisted on the wearing of masks and the use of hand sanitizer.

The minute I set foot in France I was abruptly transported into a world of science fiction. Helsinki suddenly seemed as far away as the outer edge of the solar system.

"Even today I wonder if it wasn't all a dream."

I raise my head and look at them, one after the other. I murmur that I think I have nothing left to add. They know what happened after that: France. The months of self-isolation we all went through. The stampede for toilet paper. The applause at our windows every evening at eight. Doubt, questioning. Sending resumes and cover letters you knew perfectly well no one would read. Tending the vegetable garden. The boom in online classes in relaxation and letting-go. Devouring books from the family library—the complete works of Henri Troyat or Christine Arnothy, writers no one reads anymore. Redecorating the house, making changes that my mother, from the other side of the screen, is not at all sure she likes. This same mother, her sole obsession that of getting to the bottom, at last, of what happened to me in Scandinavia. You broke up, is that it? Or worse, an abortion? I remained evasive. I assured her that in any case it wasn't anything catastrophic. Which was true, basically. I blocked

Ari and Annika on my phone and social media. They carried on with their lives without me. It was easier for everyone.

The important thing now was to follow my own desires, not other people's. To regain a semblance of control. Then along came the second, then the third wave, and I thought that, literally, I was going to go under—just as conditions were starting to be less drastic.

I walked around with documents certifying that I could leave the house, duly filled out. Every morning I left my mother's house and walked to the center of town. I really wanted to see people. Even with masks on. Even distrustful. Even aggressive. I wandered through the streets and told myself over and over that some day all this would come to an end, and on that day, the first thing I'd do would be to come and drink a coffee here, at Le Tom's. I'd sit myself down at a table toward the back. I'd get out my colored pencils and chalks and felt-tips. I'd feast on color. That was how I'd get back in touch with the world, postpandemic. That afterworld in which I did not want to live the life from before.

What was I hoping for?

No idea.

Maybe to find myself with three virtual strangers, in the middle of the night, chasing away demons by building castles in the air?

Fabrice clears his throat and tilts his head slightly to one side.

"Will you show us your drawings?"

And we smile, the two of us, then all four of us.

EPILOGUE
6:00 A.M.

JOCELYNE

I TOLD THEM I'd take care of closing up.

When you're old, you're not sleepy, even when you've spent the whole night listening to stories. As part of a sort of nocturnal gang, with people who are decades younger than you are and who, by dawn, are collapsing with fatigue. Chloé invited them to go and get some rest at her mother's place. They'll walk through town. The café will stay closed today. I'll join them in the evening. José promised he'd make us dinner.

I'll be seventy-one soon, and I've rarely felt so fulfilled. I've just handed over the keys, officially. A load off my mind. These thirtysomething kids are neither my friends, nor my family—but they're the ones who'll be with me to the end. Chloé will be giving Fabrice a hand, and he'll hire the young guy, Ahmed, that José recommended. They'll form a new team. In no time people will be saying that Le Tom's has been there forever. How do they know? That old-fashioned name, so reminiscent of the fifties or sixties. The sweet cocktails. The jazz melodies.

I'll stay here a few more weeks, probably, and then I'll take the train to the ocean. It will be crowded and I'll drink my fill of maskless faces and of smiles, visible once again.

At night I'll go for my habitual walk along the waterfront. They'll probably come in August, during those two weeks when the deserted town goes to sleep. Even José won't be able to resist my invitation. He'll say his goodbyes then leave from there, the break will be cleaner, less painful. We'll see him off at the station and he'll promise us videos and photos and conversations and voice messages, and who knows what else?

I'm about to close the iron shutter, and then I think better of it. No. I want to hear the echoes of the night's stories for a little longer, and make the most of the prospects on the horizon, while the rays of the sun begin to light up Place Urbain IV.

I'll bring out one of the tables—no, leave it, I don't need help. I'm a strong woman. One chair. Two, if you'd like to join me. I start up the coffee machine. The enticing aroma. The morning light over the town.

That's it.

Coffee on the terrace.

It's exactly what we need.

Will you join me?

JEAN-PHILIPPE BLONDEL was born in 1964 in Troyes, France, where he lives as an author and English teacher. His novels *The 6:41 to Paris* and *Exposed* have been acclaimed in both the United States and Europe.

ALISON ANDERSON is a novelist and translator. She has translated Blondel's *The 6:41 to Paris* and *Exposed* as well as works by J. M. G. Le Clézio, Christian Bobin, Muriel Barbery, and Amélie Nothomb.

EXPOSED
BY JEAN-PHILIPPE BLONDEL

A French teacher on the verge of retirement is invited to a glittering opening that showcases the artwork of his former student, who has since become a celebrated painter. This unexpected encounter leads to the older man posing for his portrait. Possibly in the nude. Such personal exposure at close range entails a strange and troubling pact between artist and sitter that prompts both to reevaluate their lives.

THE 6:41 TO PARIS
BY JEAN-PHILIPPE BLONDEL

Cécile, a stylish 47-year-old, has spent the weekend visiting her parents outside Paris. By Monday morning, she's exhausted. These trips back home are stressful and she settles into a train compartment with an empty seat beside her. But it's soon occupied by a man she recognizes as Philippe Leduc, with whom she had a passionate affair that ended in her brutal humiliation 30 years ago. In the fraught hour and a half that ensues, Cécile and Philippe hurtle towards the French capital in a psychological thriller about the pain and promise of past romance.

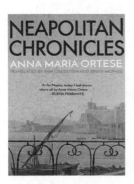

NEAPOLITAN CHRONICLES
BY ANNA MARIA ORTESE

A classic of European literature, this superb collection of fiction and reportage is set in Italy's most vibrant and turbulent metropolis—Naples—in the immediate aftermath of World War Two. These writings helped inspire Elena Ferrante's best-selling novels and she has expressed deep admiration for Ortese.

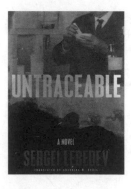

UNTRACEABLE
BY SERGEI LEBEDEV

An extraordinary Russian novel about poisons of all kinds: physical, moral and political. Professor Kalitin is a ruthless, narcissistic chemist who has developed an untraceable lethal poison called Neophyte while working in a secret city on an island in the Russian far east. When the Soviet Union collapses, he defects to the West in a riveting tale through which Lebedev probes the ethical responsibilities of scientists providing modern tyrants with ever newer instruments of retribution and control.

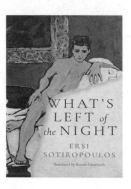

WHAT'S LEFT OF THE NIGHT
BY ERSI SOTIROPOULOS

Constantine Cavafy arrives in Paris in 1897 on a trip that will deeply shape his future and push him toward his poetic inclination. With this lyrical novel, tinged with an hallucinatory eroticism that unfolds over three unforgettable days, celebrated Greek author Ersi Sotiropoulos depicts Cavafy in the midst of a journey of self-discovery across a continent on the brink of massive change. A stunning portrait of a budding author—before he became C.P. Cavafy, one of the 20th century's greatest poets—that illuminates the complex relationship of art, life, and the erotic desires that trigger creativity.

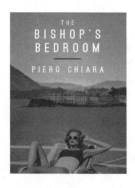

THE BISHOP'S BEDROOM
BY PIERO CHIARA

World War Two has just come to an end and there's a yearning for renewal. A man in his thirties is sailing on Lake Maggiore in northern Italy, hoping to put off the inevitable return to work. Dropping anchor in a small, fashionable port, he meets the enigmatic owner of a nearby villa. The two form an uneasy bond, recognizing in each other a shared taste for idling and erotic adventure. A sultry, stylish psychological thriller executed with supreme literary finesse.

THE EYE
BY PHILIPPE COSTAMAGNA

It's a rare and secret profession, comprising a few dozen people around the world equipped with a mysterious mixture of knowledge and innate sensibility. Summoned to Swiss bank vaults, Fifth Avenue apartments, and Tokyo storerooms, they are entrusted by collectors, dealers, and museums to decide if a coveted picture is real or fake and to determine if it was painted by Leonardo da Vinci or Raphael. *The Eye* lifts the veil on the rarified world of connoisseurs devoted to the authentication and discovery of Old Master artworks.

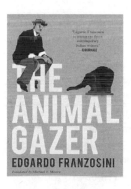

THE ANIMAL GAZER
BY EDGARDO FRANZOSINI

A hypnotic novel inspired by the strange and fascinating life of sculptor Rembrandt Bugatti, brother of the fabled automaker. Bugatti obsessively observes and sculpts the baboons, giraffes, and panthers in European zoos, finding empathy with their plight and identifying with their life in captivity. Rembrandt Bugatti's work, now being rediscovered, is displayed in major art museums around the world and routinely fetches large sums at auction. Edgardo Franzosini recreates the young artist's life with intense lyricism, passion, and sensitivity.

ALLMEN AND THE DRAGONFLIES
BY MARTIN SUTER

Johann Friedrich von Allmen has exhausted his family fortune by living in Old World grandeur despite present-day financial constraints. Forced to downscale, Allmen inhabits the garden house of his former Zurich estate, attended by his Guatemalan butler, Carlos. This is the first of a series of humorous, fast-paced detective novels devoted to a memorable gentleman thief. A thrilling art heist escapade infused with European high culture and luxury that doesn't shy away from the darker side of human nature.

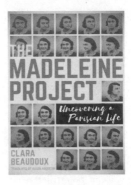

THE MADELEINE PROJECT
BY CLARA BEAUDOUX

A young woman moves into a Paris apartment and discovers a storage room filled with the belongings of the previous owner, a certain Madeleine who died in her late nineties, and whose treasured possessions nobody seems to want. In an audacious act of journalism driven by personal curiosity and humane tenderness, Clara Beaudoux embarks on *The Madeleine Project*, documenting what she finds on Twitter with text and photographs, introducing the world to an unsung 20th century figure.

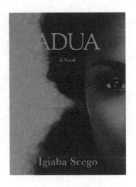

ADUA
BY IGIABA SCEGO

Adua, an immigrant from Somalia to Italy, has lived in Rome for nearly forty years. She came seeking freedom from a strict father and an oppressive regime, but her dreams of film stardom ended in shame. Now that the civil war in Somalia is over, her homeland calls her. She must decide whether to return and reclaim her inheritance, but also how to take charge of her own story and build a future.

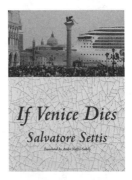

IF VENICE DIES
BY SALVATORE SETTIS

Internationally renowned art historian Salvatore Settis ignites a new debate about the Pearl of the Adriatic and cultural patrimony at large. In this fiery blend of history and cultural analysis, Settis argues that "hit-and-run" visitors are turning Venice and other landmark urban settings into shopping malls and theme parks. This is a passionate plea to secure the soul of Venice, written with consummate authority, wide-ranging erudition, and élan.

THE MADONNA OF NOTRE DAME
BY ALEXIS RAGOUGNEAU

Fifty thousand people jam into Notre Dame Cathedral to celebrate the Feast of the Assumption. The next morning, a beautiful young woman clothed in white kneels at prayer in a cathedral side chapel. But when someone accidentally bumps against her, her body collapses. She has been murdered. This thrilling novel illuminates shadowy corners of the world's most famous cathedral, shedding light on good and evil with suspense, compassion, and wry humor.

THE LAST WEYNFELDT
BY MARTIN SUTER

Adrian Weynfeldt is an art expert in an international auction house, a bachelor in his mid-fifties living in a grand Zurich apartment filled with costly paintings and antiques. Always correct and well-mannered, he's given up on love until one night—entirely out of character for him—Weynfeldt decides to take home a ravishing but unaccountable young woman and gets embroiled in an art forgery scheme that threatens his buttoned up existence. This refined page-turner moves behind elegant bourgeois facades into darker recesses of the heart.

MOVING THE PALACE
BY CHARIF MAJDALANI

A young Lebanese adventurer explores the wilds of Africa, encountering an eccentric English colonel in Sudan and enlisting in his service. In this lush chronicle of far-flung adventure, the military recruit crosses paths with a compatriot who has dismantled a sumptuous palace and is transporting it across the continent on a camel caravan. This is a captivating modern-day Odyssey in the tradition of Bruce Chatwin and Paul Theroux.

New Vessel Press

To purchase these titles and for more information
please visit newvesselpress.com.